With my

[handwritten signature]

You Also May Enjoy These Books
by
Theodore Jerome Cohen

Death by Wall Street*
House of Cards*
Lilith*
Night Shadows*
Eighth Circle*
Wheel of Fortune*
Frozen in Time†
Unfinished Business†
End Game†
Cold Blood††
Full Circle
The Hypnotist‡ ‡‡
The Road Less Taken – Books 1 & 2
Creative Ink, Flashy Fiction – Books 1, 2, 3, 4, 5 & 6
Flash Fiction for Animal Lovers (Anthology Book 7)
Flash Fiction Stories of the Young (Anthology Book 8)

* A Detective Louis Martelli, NYPD, Mystery/Thriller
† The Antarctic Murders Trilogy
†† The Antarctic Murders Trilogy (all three books)
‡ Young Adult (YA) novel written under the pen name "Alyssa Devine"
‡‡ Also available in a special paperback edition for readers with dyslexia

Visit us on the World Wide Web
http://www.theodore-cohen-novels.com
http://www.alyssadevinenovels.com

Mementos

A Unique Collection of
Short Stories & Flash Fiction
Book 1 in the <u>Mementos Anthologies</u> Series

Theodore Jerome Cohen

TJC Press

TJC Press
122 Shady Brook Drive
Langhorne, PA 19047-8027 USA
www.theodore-cohen-novels.com
© *Theodore Jerome Cohen, 2018* • *All rights reserved*

The stories in this book are works of fiction, though some were inspired by real events. Except as noted in the **Endnotes**, which are made a part of this declaration, any resemblance to actual persons (living or dead), events, or locales in the context of the stories presented here, is coincidental. All brand names and product names used in this book are trademarks, registered trademarks, or trade names of their respective holders.

Some stories first appeared as submissions to Flash Fiction Challenges sponsored by Indies Unlimited (www.IndiesUnlimited.com): these were inspired by copyrighted photographic prompts provided by K. S. Brooks that were originally posted at Indies Unlimited.

First Edition; First Printing, 2019
ISBN-10: 1727401840 (sc)
ISBN-13: 978-1-7274-0184-4 (sc)

Published in the United States of America
Front cover design by Theodore Jerome Cohen
The paperback edition is printed using THE DOVES TYPE® typeface, Robert Green's digital recreation of the Doves Press Fount of Type. See **Endnote 1** for more information.
https://typespec.co.uk/doves-type/

Photo Credits
Front cover art: czamy bez, Big Stock Photo
Frontispiece: Big Stock Photo
Photograph of Theodore Jerome Cohen: Susan Cohen, 2006
Photograph of Alyssa Devine: Big Stock Photo
Photographic prompts copyrighted by K. S. Brooks are used with permission. The copyright or other attribution associated with any given photographic prompt (e.g., royalty-free acquisitions from Big Stock Photo; public domain: etc.) is provided with that prompt. Please provide documented proof of any errors or omissions in, or any changes requested to, these prompts (e.g., changes resulting from inadvertent copyright violations), by letter, to TJC Press.

eBook created by Kindle Direct Publishing (KDP)
Printed by Kindle Direct Publishing (KDP), An Amazon.com Company
Available from Amazon.com and other retail outlets

To William Alden Lee

1933 - 2019

■

"Photography is there to construct the idea of us as a great family and we go on vacations and take these pictures and then we look at them later and we say, 'Isn't this a great family?' So, photography is instrumental in creating family not only as a memento, a souvenir, but also a kind of mythology."

Larry Sultan

∎

Table of Contents

A Note from Theodore Jerome Cohen

People ask: "Why do you use photographic prompts when you write short stories and flash fiction?" Larry Sultan, an American photographer from the San Fernando Valley in California, provides one answer: "Photography is there to construct the idea of us as a great family and we go on vacations and take these pictures and then we look at them later and we say, 'Isn't this a great family?' So, photography is instrumental in creating family not only as a memento, a souvenir, but also a kind of mythology." Beyond the physical, however, lie our memories and in them, the pictures stored in our minds' eyes. As writers, aren't these memories—both the physical and the "mementos of the mind"—the essence of our works, the prompts we use to spin the words and phrases into literary tapestries our readers can use to discover something about life, a bit about us, and, in a process, perhaps, a little about themselves?

Some of the stories found here were entered into Flash Fiction Challenges managed by the Website *Indies Unlimited*. In a nutshell, the Challenges (which begin every Saturday morning at 9 a.m., Pacific time) require participants to write a complete story (plot, characters, hook, and slam-bang finish) in 250 words or fewer. Each must incorporate the elements of a photographic and written prompt. Language and subject matter must be kept at the PG-13 level.[1] Entries are accepted until Tuesday at 5:00 p.m., with the winner announced on the following Saturday. Weekly winners, selected by popular vote, receive the "Flash Fiction Star." Another weekly winner, "Editors' Choice," is selected by the administrators/editors for inclusion in an annual anthology. Announcements of the latter can lag submission by several months.

---

[1] You can learn more at www.indiesunlimited.com/flash-fiction/

The stories here all were inspired by interesting or unusual photographs found on the Internet. And if some of the stories appear somewhat obtuse, read their associated endnotes. You may be surprised at what inspired any given tale.

Theodore Jerome Cohen
Langhorne, Pennsylvania
July 5, 2019

NB: The paperback edition of this book is printed using THE DOVES TYPE® typeface, Robert Green's digital recreation of the Doves Press Fount of Type. See **Endnote 1** for more information on this typeface and its tortured history.

Acknowledgements

A tip of the hat and many thanks to Sandy Rangel, Audience Services Volunteer, WETA TV & FM, Washington, DC, for refreshing my memory on the Off-Broadway play *Steambath* that stuck in my mind and inspired my short story, "Judgment Day."

To Retired U.S. Navy Commander William Alden Lee, my earnest—and now, regrettably, erstwhile—grammarian and long-suffering editor: thank you for ferreting out those ever-elusive typos and other errors—including my often-grievous offenses against the English language—that somehow manage to worm their way into my manuscripts' drafts. That said, I alone take full responsibility for this book's contents.

Finally, I will forever be grateful to my wife, Susan—the love of my life—who provides vital suggestions and, equally important, unswerving support, during the development of all my writings.

I don't know what I would do without you all.

Mementos

Mementos Anthology – Book 1

"Judgment Day" (Photo: autotrader)
1983 Cadillac Eldorado Coupe

So, it was strange, she thought, that on this one day—this one *terrible* day—he, for some reason, asked her to come with him. More than that, he wanted *her* to drive his rusty, beat-up Eldorado.

1. Judgment Day

NO coverage, not even one bar, the battery was dead anyway. It was still daytime, but there was an overcast and the sky had a perfectly even dullness, so there was no way to tell what time of day it was, much less which direction was north or south or anything else for that matter. A two-lane blacktop road snaked up into the distance and disappeared into some trees, or a forest if you wanted to get technical about it. It also snaked down toward some lumpy hills and disappeared there as well. What sounded like a two-stroke chainsaw could be heard in the distance, but it was impossible to tell whether it was up in the forest or down in the lumpy hills. This had been happening more often lately. Two different ways to go, with a dead battery and no bars, and nobody left to blame.[2]

His '83 Cadillac Eldorado was tilted toward its right side, the car severely damaged, with weeds and other debris entangled in the wheels and chassis. One minute they had been cruising up the two-lane blacktop—speeding would be a more accurate description—the next, they saw two deer, one a ten-point buck, standing in their path, the animals' eyes caught in the headlights of the onrushing car.

Dakota had swerved to avoid the inevitable, missing the deer but throwing the four-door sedan violently off the road. It lurched to the left and right as she fought the wheel, the car kicking up sticks and stones before finally coming to rest in the ditch adjacent to the pavement some 200 feet down the road. Now,

---

[2] This story was entered into the 2018 Owl Canyon Press Hackathon #1 of June, 2018. Here, the sponsors provided the first and 50th paragraphs (**bolded**), and participants were required to provide the 2nd through 49th paragraphs. Each paragraph was required to have at least 40 words. Alas, this entry did not win an award.

she and her passenger, Cassidy, were the ones in peril as gasoline dripped from a severed fuel line onto the car's huge 6.0-liter V-8 engine.

Somehow, Dakota and Cassidy, although knocked unconscious, managed to escape unscathed, not a scratch between them. He recovered first, shook his head, and looked at his watch. It was smashed beyond recognition. His companion appeared to be comatose. Reaching over, he gently massaged her shoulder. Dakota moaned and slowly regained consciousness. As best he could tell, they must have been out cold for hours. Who knew what time it was?!

Laboring mightily, with the smell of gasoline burning in his nostrils, Cassidy first grabbed the small box in front of him on the vehicle's floorboard and then, after crawling out the passenger-side window, worked his way around the front of the car to the driver's side and helped Dakota out. Once up the embankment and on the pavement, the pair made their way toward the sound of the chainsaw.

For some time, he'd been hearing rumors about people clearing land in the county for new home construction. Even if that weren't the case just now, *someone* was cutting timber nearby and, he said, might be able to provide assistance. Regardless, retracing their route was *not* an option; it only would take them back to where his troubles had begun, to where the bodies were buried.

As it always had been since he saved her from herself, Dakota stayed close but slightly behind him. She said nothing. Formerly homeless, and charging $20 a trick in the sleeper of any Kenworth or Peterbilt tractor she could find at the local truck stop on the interstate, she was going nowhere but down when Cassidy spotted her at a nearby diner, became a "regular," and eventually took her in. She seemed grateful for whatever he did for her.

But Dakota never was sure what Cassidy did during the day—or at night, for that matter. He came and went at all hours, never said more than a few words to her when he even bothered to show up for dinner and some mechanical love-making in his single-wide trailer on the outskirts of Northfield, and then, he was gone again, without so much as a word regarding when he might return.

So, she spent her days reading romance magazines and watching television. They simply were two people living under one roof, people whose lives intersected only occasionally and, even then, under the most superficial of conditions. He never bothered her, and she, certainly, never demanded, much less asked, anything of him.

So, it was strange, she thought, that on this one day—this one *terrible* day—he, for some reason, asked her to come with him. More than that, he wanted *her* to drive his rusty, beat-up Eldorado. All he would say was that it had to do with him wanting to take care of some unfinished business. That's what he had said.

He assured her she could handle what he often referred to as The Beast. That car, to be sure, was a behemoth. Low slung and over-powered, it lumbered down the road, gave the driver fits when turning—in general, it was a gigantic pain in the ass when it came to maneuvering in tight spaces—and always bottomed on the slightest dip in the road. Still, today, for whatever reason, Cassidy insisted that *Dakota* was to be his designated driver, her vehement protests notwithstanding!

It wasn't so much that he had insisted on her driving but the fact that he had loaded his Smith & Wesson Model 29 six-shot revolver with .44 Magnum cartridges—the same kind of gun and cartridge his idol, Clint Eastwood, used in the *Dirty Harry* movie—and had stuck it in his shoulder holster under his tan leather jacket with such an air of punitive certainty that she shuddered with apprehension. Going with him under these circumstances was to her, in a word, frightening!

Cassidy wasn't one to take *no* for an answer, especially from someone who'd been bedding down in his trailer lo these many months, not to mention having eaten the food he'd been bringing through the door. So, off they drove, she at the wheel, he riding shotgun, as it were.

Except for the occasional driving instructions he barked at her on the road out of town—sharp commands amounting to his telling her to turn right or left, or to head up this or that dirt road—Cassidy said nothing, his eyes steeled on the pavement ahead. She dared not speak, afraid even to ask where they were going or who might be there when they arrived.

She peered out the corner of her eye and saw Cassidy bouncing his left leg up and down: a sign of his nervousness. This made her even more anxious, and the farther they drove from his trailer, the more her anticipation turned to dread.

It was an hour after they had left his trailer and roughly ten minutes after he had ordered her to turn right onto a washboard road the county long ago had forgotten to grade that he ordered her to stop. Her apprehension was heightened when she saw what Cassidy did next. Removing the Model 29 revolver from its holster, he spun the chamber and, apparently satisfied, placed the revolver on his lap and ordered her to turn right again.

The road, now, if it even could be called that, comprised two puddled, muddy tracks through weeded land leading to a ramshackle shack with a tin roof and a weather-beaten porch on which stood two men in coveralls. Each was holding a shotgun leveled at the oncoming car. A large black Labrador stood to one side. Cassidy put his right hand out the window and waved. The men lowered their guns.

Dakota pulled the car in front of the shack, stopped, and on Cassidy's order, killed the engine. Then, he—without warning—opened the passenger-side door, exited, and opened fire, shooting the two men and the dog dead before they even knew what hit them. Three shots, each one right between the eyes. Dakota threw up over herself and the steering wheel.

Tossing the revolver onto the front seat, Cassidy ordered Dakota out of the car and, grabbing her by the arm, forced her to walk with him to the shed behind the shack. Inside, he found a spade, thrust it into her hand, picked up another for himself, and, after dragging the men and the dog to a damp area in the woods near the property's fence line, dug three shallow graves and buried the trio in order to keep vultures and bears from scavenging the bodies. Dakota, shaking and still in shock, said nothing.

A strong smell of ammonia hung in the air, something akin to cat urine or rotten eggs. Yet, she saw no cats . . . the black Lab surely would have made short work of them if there had been any, she thought. Still, she was sure *something* close by was responsible for the odor.

Dakota wrinkled her nose, gagged, and threw up again. Seeing that, Cassidy laughed, thrust his large kerchief into her hand, and, yelling at her to cover her nose and mouth, belittled her for not having the stomach to handle the stench from the property's meth lab.

He grabbed the shovel from her hand, ordered her back to the car, and told her to clean herself and the car. He also berated her for being so weak as to get sick at the sight of him killing two men who, by his measure, had tried to cheat

6

him and who would have killed him—and her—if he hadn't acted first! It was the way things were done in his world, he said.

And with that, he tromped up the front steps, entered the shack, and began ransacking the front room. Through the open door, Dakota saw him overturning furniture, tearing up the floorboards with a crowbar, and pulling down bookcases before turning his attention to the rear of the structure.

It was when he went into the kitchen that she heard him doing the most damage. The noise emanating from that room was continuous and almost deafening, largely metallic in nature and accompanied by the occasional sounds of glass and pottery breaking and of furniture being overturned. Whatever Cassidy was searching for, it was well-hidden.

Within minutes he returned to the car, a small cardboard box in his hand and a grim but satisfied look on his face. He told her not to ask him questions about what he was holding. Then, he ordered her to start the engine, turn the Eldorado around, and drive back to the main highway as fast as she could.

Dakota did as she was told. Looking in the rearview mirror, she was startled to see an orange glow from what appeared to be a fire consuming the shack from which Cassidy, not minutes earlier, had exited. Whatever business he had had with the two men, it obviously had been concluded, totally and finally.

They pressed on until he told her where to make one final turn, putting them back on the two-lane blacktop road. Now, however, they were heading *out* of the county. At his urging, she pressed the accelerator to the floor.

The Eldorado lurched forward, crested the next hill—the exhaust pipe and muffler scraping the asphalt—and came face-to-face with a ten-point buck and doe, their eyes staring directly into the headlights of the oncoming car. Dakota instinctively swung the steering wheel to the right. It would be the last thing she remembered doing until she and Cassidy woke up in the ditch, presumably much later.

Now, they found themselves on foot, not knowing where they were or how to get help. Dakota also silently wondered about the box Cassidy was carrying. What was in it, and why was it so important to him that he killed two men and their dog for it? This much she did know, however: whatever was in the box, she wanted nothing to do with it!

They walked for the better part of what seemed like an hour, the sound of the chainsaw fading with each step they took until it finally stopped completely. As well, the sun was setting. Strangely, no cars passed them in all that time—not one, in *either* direction. Yet, in spite of having thought otherwise earlier, this appeared to be a county road, one both well-maintained and signed.

In the encroaching dullness of the evening fog, the only light that could be seen was what appeared to be a flashing neon sign on the other side of a hill up ahead—a flashing neon sign for the Sky Bowl Lanes bowling alley, a sign barely visible through a stand of pines and dense undergrowth that took on even more ominous proportions as the sky grew dark.

Cassidy ordered Dakota to follow him, shaking his head in disbelief while noting aloud that in all the years he'd lived in the area, he'd never heard of, much less seen, a bowling alley where they stood. Yet, there it was, right in front of them, with a huge bowling pin outlined in blue neon atop the building and the words "Sky Bowl" emblazed in white neon across the bowling pin.

They made their way to the building, passing several cars parked in the lot to its front. Once in the building, they saw that only a few lanes were occupied, mostly by two or more elderly men playing leisurely games—men who didn't seem to be in any hurry to roll the ball or mark their scores.

Women, too, could be found bowling on various lanes, but they were the exception. They also appeared to be playing at a leisurely pace. It was as if everyone were waiting for something to happen, and the games were meant to pass the time as opposed to being ends unto themselves.

Cassidy shrugged and ordered Dakota to follow him to the shoe counter, where he apprised the attendant of the fact that he, Cassidy, must have fallen asleep, had driven his car into the ditch, and needed to use the phone to call for a tow truck.

The counterman, smiling, apologized but stated that, unfortunately, their phone was out of order. Cassidy looked at him incredulously, wondering aloud how an obviously well-established business could be without telephone service. The attendant shrugged, noting that few among its patrons were those who even had need of a telephone. Besides, he asked, would Cassidy and his lady friend like to bowl a few games just to pass the time until their situation could be sorted out?

Cassidy looked puzzled by this question, but before he and Dakota could make sense of it, the attendant was asking about their shoe sizes—about what size bowling shoes he and his lady friend wore. Cassidy had a dazed look on his face.

Unsure as to what exactly was happening, Cassidy stared at the attendant and stated that he had been down the nearby two-lane road a thousand times in his life and had *never* even seen the bowling alley from the highway.

The counterman, smiling, assured him they had been there for a long time—in fact, he stated they had been here for an eternity and then some—whereupon he leaned over the counter, eyed Cassidy's shoes, and again asked him what size shoe he wore. Then, he pleasantly suggested, as before, that Cassidy and his lady friend bowl a few games while they waited.

Cassidy grew angry. He insisted on knowing for *what* they were waiting. He only needed to make one phone call—to a towing company, he asserted—and then, once the tow truck arrived, they would be on their way. There was no need to spend any more time in the bowling alley. There was no need of bowling shoes. All they needed was a working phone.

Again, Cassidy asked the counterman what they were waiting for. The man, looking Cassidy in the eye, told him not to be so impatient, that life was too short to worry about everything getting done this minute, and oh, by the way, he should try these shoes—that he looked to be about a size 12.

Cassidy now was stumbling over his words—babbling would be a better description. In fact, he was becoming unhinged, unable to grasp what was happening at the counter as the attendant handed him a pair of bowling shoes and, leaning over the counter, began sizing up Dakota's shoe requirements.

Smiling, he turned, walked to the rack behind the counter, and selected a pair of new, pink, size-6 shoes. Returning to the counter, he handed them to Dakota, remarking that there never was a charge at the Sky Bowl Lanes.

Dakota stepped back, sat, and put on the shoes. Cassidy, however, clutching the box he had taken earlier in the day and his bowling shoes, still was not satisfied. He asserted he was *not* worried, only confused. He simply didn't understand what was going on.

The attendant smiled. He told Cassidy that everything will be clear in due time, and, citing *Thessalonians 4:17*, recalled that those who are alive, who were left, will be caught up together with them in the clouds to meet the Lord in the air, and so, would always be with Him.

Cassidy backed away from the counter, stating he wasn't so sure he liked what he was hearing. But the counterman assured him that he had nothing to fear. Then, as if to reassure him further, he motioned for Cassidy to look out the front window of the bowling alley, toward the line of vehicles parked in front.

Cassidy could not believe his eyes. There, parked in the first spot by the door, was his prized '83 Eldorado, gleaming in the bright lights of the establishment's sign and parking lot lamps. The car appeared new, as if it had been driven off the dealer's lot only minutes before. Gone was the rust. Gone were any signs it had been mired in the ditch alongside the two-lane blacktop road only hours earlier, when it had been ensnared in the brush with its right side and chassis severely scratched and damaged. It was as if the car had been reborn to once again relive its glory days.

Tears streamed down Cassidy's cheeks as he stared out the window and watched as a crowd assembled admiringly around his car. Inside, others gathered around him and Dakota to marvel at the sight of the vehicle and to congratulate them on what their eyes beheld.

Still, the counterman saw fear in Cassidy's and Dakota's eyes. He knew they either did not, or could not, comprehend what they were seeing. So, he cautioned them not to be afraid. Putting his arms around their shoulders, he told them both, gently, that the die had been cast, and for them, there was no turning back.

They made their way through the crowd, and back to the Eldorado. And as they approached it, a crow flew directly over their heads and landed on the hood and then looked at them. They stood some distance away and watched the crow watching them. Another crow flew directly overhead and landed beside it. The first crow squawked and then both flew away. They watched the crows disappear, looked at each other, and then got in the Eldorado. Only one way to go this time, with five bars and full battery.

See Endnote 2.

"Ashley's Revenge" (Photo: holbox; Big Stock Photo)

The only sounds that could be heard were the ebb and flow
of the surf and the occasional seagull overhead.

2. Ashley's Revenge

It was the trumpets that alerted her to the prince's impending arrival—three short blasts, like the sound from a shofar on Rosh Hashanah—and then, a fanfare, his usual tribute, which always sent the royal guards scurrying in preparation for His Highness's grand entrance. Ashley sprang from the floor, which was covered in pillows, and, dismissing her three servants, who disappeared out the back of the tent, flung herself through the front flaps in time to see her lover, his long black hair flowing in the wind, galloping over the dunes on a magnificent white stallion, the animal's nostrils flaring, as the two bore down on the encampment near the Arabian Sea. The prince reined in his steed and, throwing his right leg over the horse's head, gracefully dismounted, rushed to Ashley's side, and swept her into his arms. Carrying her into his tent, he tore her silken garments from her body and made mad, passionate love to her as he never had before. Afterwards, she bathed in her tent, attended by handmaidens who combed her hair and perfumed her body in preparation for a midnight horseback ride over the desert floor with the prince. *I wonder what that bitch Ellice Hamilton would think if she could see me now,* she thought. *She thinks she's so smart, always with the name-calling and sneaky little tricks. Like the time she said Trey was waiting for me at the corner of 82nd and Madison, which he wasn't, while she and that mouse Brittany Davidson stood there and laughed as I waited like an idiot for 30 minutes.*

She looked up, startled to see him. I thought you had gone home for the night, she whispered. You must be kidding, he replied, stepping into her private office, pulling the blinds, and removing his tie and shirt. There's no one here but you and me, he said. The cleaning crew seems to have finished and left the floor. Best of all, Ellice is in Chicago, visiting her mother, who's in the hospital. He gave her "that look." She bit her lower lip and pushed her chair back. In an instant he was at her side, sweeping everything from her desk, and laying her gently across its glass top. Ripping her blouse away, he kissed her arched body until she thought she would never be able to breathe again, whereupon they made love through the night until the sun rose above the horizon. *Ha! I hope someone pulls that on Ellice when she's married. That'll pay her back for sending notes around, telling everyone how I have a crush on Trey and how I hope he'll invite me to the Halloween dance this fall. What a bitch she is. She and her little pet Brittany pretending to be my friend, stopping by the apartment to invite me to walk up 81st Street to school one day and then, turning on me the next.*

Trey had rented the cottage on the beach in the Hamptons for her a year earlier, and now, as the week was coming to a close, the anticipation was almost too much for her to bear. After all, it had been a week of relaxing on the deserted beach, reading and sunning, all without him. But the waiting soon would be over. It was Friday, and as the sun was setting, she heard a car door slam. Turning around, she saw him running toward her through a narrow path in the tall beach grass, his open shirt flapping in the breeze as the wind blew his straw hat back into the brush. They flung themselves into each other's arms, he smothering her in kisses while she threw her head back, eyes closed, drinking in the very essence of his soul. In an instant, he carried her to the blanket she had spread on the sand that morning, and, for what seemed an eternity, they made passionate love before falling asleep in each other's arms. The only sounds that could be heard were the ebb and flow of the surf and the occasional seagull overhead. *That bitch Ellice should never have it so good,* she thought. *She certainly doesn't deserve anything like this, that's for sure, especially for the way she and that little weasel Brittany have been treating me! I saw what they did in art class last semester, make figures out of clay that looked like human heads, then pointing at me and punching the heads in the face. I'll punch them in the face one of these days—I'll give them both knuckle sandwiches, that's what I'll do. It'll serve them right!*

"Ashley. Ashley!"

"Yes, Mother?"

"Put your action figure dolls away. It's time to leave."

"Aw, Mother, just five more minutes, please."

"I'm sorry, honey, your Father's already loaded the car. And besides, we're due at the Teitelbaums' for dinner tonight. Trey'll be there too, ya know. But we'll be back in the Hamptons next weekend. Come on. Time's a-wastin'."

"A Final Goodbye" (Photo: Wikipedia; public domain)
Steamboat Sultana at Helena, Arkansas, on April 26, 1865,
a day before her destruction. A crowd of paroled
prisoners covers her decks.

*Dear Pa I hury to rite a few lins befor we bored the
steembote Sultana for the trip north.*

3. A Final Goodbye

April 21, 1865

Dear Pa I hury to rite a few lins befor we bored the steembote Sultana for the trip north. I am tolerbly wel despite a yer spent in Andersonvil under the most horible condisons yu can imagin. We was lured into a trap last spring by the Rebs who deraled are train and caused the engine to blow up. It was a horible site with the enginer and fireman bodys blown apart. In all, 10 men out of 50 in our Regiment was kilt and 20 more injured, including Jesse Lathrop—yu remember him, he worked on the farm down the rode from us. He was hurt sumthing bad and so was his son. Maybe by now yu herd Bill Joseph bin kilt. His Regiment was shot all to peaces. I dont know what hapened to his son Temple. The last we saw he was marched away at the point of a bayonet but we never seen him in Andersonvil so I think the Rebs kilt him. Anyway, Jesse and his son are with me in Vicksburg at the parol camp waiting to be relesed to the Union Army but they are not in gud conditon. The Sultana is a butiful bote all rite. Yu shud see her with her 2 smokestaks. I herd tel the gummint said it wud pay Captain Mason $5 for each enlisted man and $10 for evry oficer he took onbored and brott north. But first we haf to get one of the boilers fixed. The bote had gon south to New Orleans to spred word about Lincolns assasination. Isnt that terible? Rite at the end of the war to. Wen the bote was returning to pick us up, a boiler sprung a leke. A enginer is making som repares now. I do wory thogh bout the larg number of prisners Captain Mason wants to put onbored. Yu no me, I aint no gud with numbers but it seems like ther are to many prisnors waiting here—maybe 1000—wanting to go home and one oficer said the bote cud cary only 400. I sur hope hes wrong becase it wud be horible if we had an acident and men who are wunded or sick cud not get off in time to save there lives. Ples tell Ma I stil hav the Bible and comb she gav me wen I went to War. I cant wait to get bak to Michigan. Give aunt Mary and uncle Joe my respects. See yu soon. Yur luving son,

Jeremiah Peters

See Endnote 3.

"Cursed" (Photo: Pinterest)

I tol' you: he done seen an alligator crawl under Philomine's house on da day before she die. You know wha' *dat* mean!"

4. Cursed

"T ha's wha' Abraham Duval done tol' me a year ago," Sophronia Beliveau asserted as she sat sipping iced tea with her best friend, Jacqueline Rivière. It was early afternoon in Palmetto, Louisiana. The temperature already was 100 in the kitchen of the weather-beaten shack four miles west of the old concrete bridge over the Atchafalaya River.

"Abraham Duval? Who's he, woman?" Jacqueline demanded, pulling her head back and staring at her companion.

"Oh, come on, I done tol' you 'bout him at da time. You mus' be goin' senile or sumpin'. He dat ole Creole who used ta cut Philomine's grass. I tol' you: he done seen an alligator crawl under Philomine's house on da day before she die. You know wha' *dat* mean!"

"Now I 'member. Terrible t'ing, all right. Dat family be cursed for sure."

"Hush, woman . . . der're spirits about!"

"I'm just sayin," whispered Jacqueline, putting down her glass, " 'member Philomine's son, Otis?"

"You mean dat big clumsy man ever'body call *Grand Beedé*?"

"Yeah, dat's 'im, da one whose mouth was crooked 'cause he always slept wit' da Moon shinin' on 'is face. He was cursed, too. Look what happen ta *him*!"

"I know," replied Sophronia, shaking her head. "Dat boy was born under a bad sign. Can ya imagine what musta gone through Philomine's head when da State Police found 'im drowned in da bayou west of Levee Road dat mornin', 'xactly like what Madam Ophelia said wud happen?"

"See! Jus' as I said! Cursed! And look at Philomine's daughter—what's 'er name?"

"Leonie Mercier?" replied Sophronia.

"Dat's 'er. Leonie! Married 15 years to dat *bon rien* of a man, Rémy, before she finally wise' up an' t'rew 'im out. Man couldn't hold a job for longer 'an six

19

months. 'Goodbye and good riddance,' she say after she divorce' 'im. Best t'ing she ever done. But by da time he outta da house, 'er daughter Ida done pretty much picked up 'er daddy's bad habits. And dat's when t'ings really come apart at da seams."

"Dat's what I heard, too," replied Sophronia, getting up to open another window and let what passed for fresh air into the kitchen. "Yesterday, for example, I was over at Madam Ophelia's—you know, dat woman on the north side of Lebeau who does dem tarot card readings—"

"Say what?"

"You heard me!"

"I tho't you gave up wantin' to know your future, woman!" Jacqueline said, setting her glass on the table.

"Well, I did, for da mos' part. But da t'ing is, dese visits give me a chance ta catch up on *other* people's futures."

"Like who?" Jacqueline asked, sitting straight up.

"Well, if you must know: Ida's."

"You're kiddin', right?"

"No siree. Madam Ophelia, she done tol' me Leonie been to see her da day before and was askin' 'bout Ida, who, ya know, moved to Ponchatoula."

"I know. But come on, come on, tell me da rest!"

"Well, Leone wanted to know wat gonna happen ta Ida 'cause of how much trouble she always been at home."

"I know, dat girl was nothin' *but* trouble, Sophronia. 'Member how willful she was as a chil' and how it got worse after Rémy left?"

"I 'member, woman! Once Rémy gone, dat Ida gal went wild, always stayin' out late, drinkin' and havin' sex, sometimes with men 10 years older dan her. I don't know how Leonie even kept her in school."

"On top of dat, dat no good Rémy always took Ida's side, sendin' 'er money so's she could buy fancy clothes and stuff."

"An' 'member dat Saturday night in Ida's senior year of high school when Leonie and Ida had dat knock-down, drag-out fight over car keys dat sent Leonie to the hospital wit' a gash over her right eye and Ida to juvenile detention?!"

"I do," said Jacqueline, nodding, as she took a handkerchief from her purse and began mopping her brow. "So, what did Madam Ophelia say?"

"Well, it wasn't good, dat's for sure. She dealt Leonie *The Fool*, the *Eight of Wands*, *The Devil*, the *Seven of Swords*, and . . . well—"

"Really? *Really?!* You're not gonna tell me da last card?"

[Sophronia hesitated.] "*Death.*"

Jacqueline clasped both hands to her mouth. "I tol' ya. I DONE TOL' YA! Dat family be cursed!"

Sophronia shook her head. "Ida was doomed from da day she be born."

"She's a fool," cried Jacqueline. "And da way men be draggin' 'er down wit' drugs an' sex an' all, it's jus' a matter of time before da State Police come knockin' on *Leonie's* door."

"Ain't gonna happen, woman!" lamented Sophronia.

"What you talkin' 'bout?"

"I was at Surette's meat market in Lebeau when dey opened dis mornin' and ran into Alzophine LaPomeret at da counter. She done told me she saw an alligator crawl under Leonie's house not 15 minutes before she got to da market."

See Endnote 4.

Portrait of Emily Davison, ca. 1910-1912, British suffragette,
who ran in front of the King's horse at the 1913 Epsom Derby.
(Photo: Wikimedia Commons, public domain)

"She appears to 'ave thrown 'erself in front of George the Fifth's
'orse today at the Derby."

5. Trampled

"Oh

my God, Sylvia! That makes no sense!"

"I know, Emmeline. It's unbelievable. But it's true. She appears to 'ave thrown 'erself in front of George the Fifth's 'orse today at the Derby."

[Emmeline Pethick-Laurence clasps her hands to her mouth.] "I knew she was passionate about the Movement, but to commit suicide? And yes, i' makes no sense. I took 'er to the railroad station this mornin' and watched as she purchased 'er round-trip tickets for Epsom. She 'ad every intention o' returning to Victoria this afternoon."

"Well, from where I was standin', Emmeline, i' looked like she knew *exactly* wha' she was doin'. She obviously was familiar wi' the horses and the colours o' the riders' silks. Even so, there would be no missin' the red sleeves and blue body o' the jockey wearin' the King's colours, that's for sure."

"So, what 'appened, Sylvia?"

"It was as they was comin' aroun' Tattenham Corner, goin' into the final straight. She slipped under the rail, stepped in front of *Anmer*, put up 'er hands, and stood 'er ground as the 'orse 'it 'er at a full gallop. But i' was what was *in* 'er 'ands that intrigues me."

"In 'er 'ands? What did she 'ave in 'er 'ands?"

"A scarf in the suffragettes' colours."

"Wha' was she goin' to do wi' that?"

"Stuff it in *Anmer's* bridle, I think. Can you imagine the King's embarrassment if 'is 'orse crossed the finish line carrin' *our* colours?"[3]

---

[3] This story was accepted by the British literary journal Bunbury Magazine for their November, 2018, issue (Number 21). November, 2018, marks the 100th anniversary of the Suffragette Movement in England.

"'Till Death Do Us Part" (Photo: Brilliantflashfiction)

"Pull, you cursed dogs!" shouted the captain."

6. 'Till Death Do Us Part

"**P**ull, you cursed dogs!" shouted the captain as two members of the *Seawitch's* crew rowed from the treasure cave and around the point to where their pirate ship was anchored. Captain Jack Pierce, glaring, sat in the stern, his arms folded across his belly, his hands firmly gripping the pair of matched flintlock pistols tucked in his sash.

Not that Pierce was expecting his small crew to mutiny. To a man, the *Seawitch's* crew of one-hundred-and-three, from the first mate to the lowest powder monkey, respected the one-eyed pirate, a man who never flinched from a fight and always was first over the rail when they finally pulled alongside and boarded their quarry.

Booty, divided fairly, made up for their lives on the run. Still, the crew understood that penalties for insubordination or other infractions would be administered without mercy. Floggings were common. That said, depending on how long it had been since discipline was enforced, and for the express purpose of occasionally reaffirming the point that 'I, Jack Pierce, hold your life in my hands!', the captain never passed up an opportunity to punish an innocent man.

No mere walking the plank for that poor soul. No, One-Eyed Jack Pierce always found a better way to "impress" the crew: perhaps he'd sell the poor fellow to a slave trader or maroon him on an island. Or, if he was in a particularly cruel mood, it was not beyond him to keelhaul the individual, a good way, Pierce once averred to his navigator, to scrape the barnacles from the underbelly of the ship.

Thus, no one should have been surprised to hear two shots ring out as the small boat approached the *Seawitch*.

"Mutiny," shouted Jack. But it was *dead men tell no tales* that he thought.

"Cynthia" (Photo: Pinterest)

There she was, now wearing a blue dress cut well above the knees
with a top that barely concealed how well-endowed
the good Lord had made her.

7. Cynthia

"**H**old up! Hold the door!"

I had barely locked my car on the 2nd level of the parking garage when I saw the elevator doors closing.

Someone—I know not who—punched the "Open" button, revealing a conveyance already bursting at the seams.

"Room for one more?" I asked, not waiting for an answer. I backed into the elevator, holding my briefcase in front of me.

With a little jostling, using baby steps to move their bodies side-to-side and to the rear, the tightly packed group parted the way around my intruding backside until the elevator doors—alternately opening and partially closing—fully closed, but not before the car buzzed one final, angry warning.

The elevator proceeded up to the 1st parking level. There, the doors opened, but with the car full, they closed after a moment's hesitancy, and the car proceeded up, to deliver its passengers to their destinations.

"Floor?" a young man dressed in a black, three-piece pinstripe suit asked, looking at me.

"Oh, it's already punched. The 25th," I said; "a way to go yet."

"Right," he replied, and returned his gaze upward, to the ceiling, to where everyone else was staring. I kept my gaze forward.

Then, I felt arms around me, totally encircling my chest. "I was the one who pressed our floor, Mr. Lawrence," a voice cooed into my left ear.

It was Cynthia Palmer, my secretary and a flirt by any definition of the word. Just 20, this transplant from the hills of West Virginia to the halls of one of the most prestigious criminal and civil law firms in all of Northern Virginia could, at once, be both the most sophisticated woman to grace the corporate suite and, on the other hand, the most beguiling example of *femme fatale* known to man.

"Hmmm . . . is that Jovan Musk you're wearing this morning?" she asked, taking a deep breath. "I *love* that scent. It drives me *absolutely* wild!"

27

The women on either side of her edged away, obviously embarrassed by her brash behavior.

I rolled my eyes. This was par for the course, something I had come to expect from Cynthia in moments such as this. It was a game with her, to see how far she could push the envelope before I'd break out laughing. We both knew nothing would come of it. The first time she had propositioned me in my office, I picked up my telephone handset and said I thought it was a great idea, but I'd have to get my wife's permission first. At that point, we became the best of friends.

The youngest of six children—her sister, Kathleen, preceded her by a year while four boys had been born earlier—Cynthia saw her brothers, one by one, take jobs in Little Fork's coal mines even before they had finished high school. *Marching off to their deaths, they are,* she thought each morning as she saw them leave the house where her mother dutifully had packed their lunch buckets the night before. She was certain it was only a matter of time before they, like their father before them, would die of black lung disease. Even now, 10 years after his death, she still could "hear" her father's labored breathing, his shortness of breath and chronic cough, and his inability to breathe lying flat. For him, death could not have come too soon.

Guilty though she felt for leaving her widowed mother as she did, it was more than she could bear to watch her brothers follow in her father's footsteps. She knew they—and any future husband she might have—almost certainly would meet the same fate. Convincing her sister their only salvation was to leave Little Fork or end up like their mother, mourning the deaths of poor, down-on-their-luck miners who, like those in that old Tennessee Ernie Ford song "Sixteen Tons" would die owing their souls to the company store, the pair moved to Northern Virginia. Cynthia immediately set about taking secretarial courses at a local community college while Kathleen—with whom she lived and who supported the pair—tended bar at The Twisted Moose, a tavern on the Potomac River waterfront in Old Town Alexandria. Here, Kathleen met Brian, a handsome musician who regularly provided entertainment in the tavern on weekends. Within six months they were married, taking up residence in Del Ray, to where Cynthia moved as well. Six months later, Kathleen and Brian were "expecting."

Following the completion of two semesters' classes, Cynthia—or Cyn, as she was known to her friends—armed with her newly acquired secretarial skills and dressed in a skimpy red dress, succeeded on her first interview in securing a job as a legal secretary at my employer, the firm of Borchert, Simpson, and Overly, Attorneys at Law. What she knew about the law you could put in a thimble; however, the interviewer, a young man just out of college himself, could have cared less. I posit he had barely looked into Cynthia's eyes, much less at her face, during her entire interview.

Just my luck, I thought when he brought her down the hall on her first day, introduced us, showed her to a desk outside my and two other lawyers' offices, and, winking at her, returned to his office on the floor beneath ours. There she was, now wearing a blue dress cut well above the knees with a top that barely concealed how well-endowed the good Lord had made her. Frankly, she looked more like someone who was about to step out on a date than report for her first day of work at a major law firm. *Where does Human Resources come up with these people?!* I thought. *Can she even type?*

It was an hour before I heard a soft knock on the door.

"Come in."

It was Cynthia.

"Do you need something typed, Mr. Marshall?"

"No, not at this time, Miss Palmer. But you might want to familiarize yourself with the style we use for filing papers with the various courts in the area when we're defending clients on various cases."

I swiveled my chair around and, opening the file cabinet behind me, pulled a recent case file from the lowest drawer: <u>United States v. Caufield, 1976</u>.

"Here," I said, handing her the thick file. "Why don't you go through these papers and get a feeling for the types of pleadings we have to submit. This one is for a case we won two years ago in federal court over in Alexandria.

She took the file from my outstretched hand, thanked me, shut the door, and returned to her desk. I didn't hear from her the rest of the morning. When I left for lunch, I saw she had court papers and briefs spread over her entire desk. When I returned, she was still there, apparently not having eaten. I left for county court at 2 p.m. She still was going through the various documents.

When I returned early the next morning, her desk was clear. On my desk I found a note, indicating she had returned the file to the proper drawer in my cabinet and appreciated the opportunity to review the material.

Cynthia arrived for work that morning around 8:00 a.m. She knocked on my door, asked if I wanted a cup of coffee—I already had a cup—and wondered if I had a minute.

"Sure, c'mon in," I said, getting up and moving to the small conference center in my office near the panoramic window overlooking the Iwo Jima Memorial and the southern entrance to the Nation's Capital. Our building was at the eastern end of Rosslyn, just south of the Orange Line's Metro Station. The view was incredible.

"Whadja wanna talk about?" I asked, carefully sipping the steaming cup of black coffee I had poured moments earlier.

"That criminal case you gave me to look at yesterday . . . I'm curious. Howja come up with using the Fourth Amendment as your defense?"

Her question took me by surprise. For someone who had no legal training and, frankly, was expected only to take my scribblings and turn them into draft court filings for the other partners to review and mark up, her interest in the law startled me.

"Well," I began, "it was simply a matter of following the evidence trail. I mean, the police had no business searching our client's home without a warrant . . . that they even were in his home was a travesty. It was a clear case of unreasonable search and seizure. And we proved it! The fact is, it took the jury all of twenty minutes to return a verdict of Not Guilty. I'm surprised the judge didn't throw the prosecutors out of his courtroom after we finished questioning the arresting officer!"

She laughed, took a sip of her coffee, and rose. "Do ya mind if I read through some of the other cases in my spare time, Mr. Marshall?"

"Call me Bill, and the answer is: 'No, I don't mind.' You're welcome to review any of the files, but as you know, they must remain in the office at all times."

"That won't be a problem."

She turned and walked to her desk, where she began her day's work.

Talk about typing. Man, that woman could type, often beating out my documents at speeds in excess of 120 words per minute on her IBM Selectric.

And when it came time to produce correspondence to the courts or clients, she wasn't satisfied until my letters—and the letters she prepared for the two other lawyers for whom she worked—were error-free! No Wite-Out or correction tape for her! The letters had to be typed *error-free*, or she started all over again with a fresh sheet of linen stationery.

Not that Cyn was without her faults. Mondays could be particularly difficult, given her tendency to—shall we say—overdo it on the weekends. Her relationships were characterized by a steady stream of lovers. "This guy's the one, Bill," she'd say after arriving late from time to time on a Monday morning, describing someone she had met—and, most likely, slept with—that weekend, only to dump him within a month or two, if he even lasted that long.

But she never let her love life and the turmoil it brought interfere with her work . . . until that one fateful Friday in the middle of June, 1979, when she failed to show up for work.

None of the women with whom she chatted at the office had heard from her. Nor did she leave a message on my phone.

By mid-morning I was worried. A call to her sister's apartment only brought forth the answering machine. To avoid raising concerns, I left an innocuous message, something to the effect "Miss Palmer, this is Mr. Marshall. I'm calling from the courthouse to remind you, as you requested, to bring that file you took home back to the office. Thanks."

By late morning, I was *really* worried.

Then, just before noon, my phone rang.

"Bill, please come to Alexander's Three. You know, the penthouse restaurant. It's just up Wilson Boulevard. Can you be here in 10 minutes? It's important."

"Sure. Are you all right?"

"Not really. I'll tell you when you get here."

I dropped everything and hastily made my way to the parking garage, got in my car, and drove up the hill to the restaurant. Within a few minutes I had parked, taken the elevator to the penthouse, and joined Cynthia at the bar. I signaled the bartender for my usual—a Black Russian—and sat next to her.

At first, she said nothing, staring straight ahead at her image in the huge mirror in front of us.

The bartender set my drink down and left. "Cheers," I said, lifting my glass before taking a sip. "Now, what's this all about?"

She inhaled deeply on her cigarette, and then, looking up and closing her eyes, slowly blew the smoke out from between her lips.

"I'm pregnant."

The words hung in the air with the smoke from her cigarette.

I was stunned. Yes, I always knew Cyn walked on the wild side, but I figured, if she wasn't "on the pill," at least she made sure her dates took precautions.

I couldn't believe what I was hearing. I didn't even *want* to believe what I was hearing.

"Okay," I said in a measured tone, "do you know who the father is?"

She ashed her cigarette with studied deliberation into a nearby black porcelain ashtray. Then, looking down, she murmured, "It's Kathleen's husband, Brian."

"Are you sure?"

"Oh, yes. It happened a little over a month ago, on a Saturday night. Kathleen had off, so she and some of her girlfriends went into Washington to paint the town. I ditched my date around midnight, returned to the apartment we share, and paid their babysitter. Brian got home around one in the morning. We had more to drink than we should have, and one thing led to another—"

I didn't respond.

"Well, aren't you going to say something?" she demanded. "Like, how I disappointed you? Or, look at the mess I've made of things? They have a baby, for Christ's sake!"

"I'm not going to judge you, Cyn. I'm sure you'll be harder on yourself than anyone else ever could."

She took another cigarette from her pack, pounded it on her wrist, and putting the filtered end between her lips, ignited her butane lighter, and lit up. Then, after inhaling deeply, she slowly pushed the smoke out of her mouth with her tongue while inhaling through her nose.

"I can't keep the baby, you know. I can't let anyone else even know I'm pregnant. It would destroy my family, Bill. What am I going to do?"

"Do you want me to set up an appointment for you with my doctor? I'm sure he'll see you and help make whatever 'arrangements' you might want to make."

"I can't keep the baby," she repeated, as if she hadn't heard me. "I don't know what to do. I'm so sorry I got you involved."

She became flustered, stubbed her cigarette in the ashtray, and ran from the bar.

I paid the check and dashed after her, but by the time I reached the elevators, she had vanished. I couldn't call her sister's apartment, so at this point, there was nothing I could do but wait until Monday morning and continue our conversation at work.

But Cyn didn't show up for work on Monday morning. However, waiting for me when I arrived from court around 11 a.m. was a man who identified himself as Detective Masters."

"Mr. Lawrence? Mr. Bill Lawrence?"

"Yes, can I help you?"

"I'm Detective Wayne Masters of the Arlington County Police Department. I'm afraid I have some bad news, sir. Your secretary, Miss Palmer—"

"Yes?"

"She's dead."

"Cynthia? Dead?"

"Yes, sir. She apparently committed suicide last night. It looks like she jumped from the top of Alexander's Three restaurant in Rosslyn. We found your business card in her purse."

"Did she leave a note, Detective?"

"No, sir. Her sister and brother-in-law are at a total loss to explain what happened. We were hoping you, perhaps, might be able to share some thoughts regarding her state of mind."

"Beats the heck outta me, Detective. I haven't the slightest idea why the poor woman took her life."

"Stacked Pebbles" (Photo: K. S. Brooks)
Indies Unlimited, September 22, 2018

"Whoa, will ya look at these, will ya?!"

8. Stacked Pebbles

"**W**hoa, will ya look at these, will ya?!" Allison shouted to me as she crested the ridge in the Grand Tetons."

We'd been hiking since dawn, finally reaching the Teton Crest and the spectacular Jedediah Smith Wilderness.

"What is it?" I yelled, struggling to keep up with her.

"Two little piles of stones," she shouted back.

"Oh sheesh," I mumbled as I finally caught up with her. We'd taken a path far removed from any trail marked on our map—something we preferred doing when hiking the backcountry—and finding these little stacks, not true cairns, by any stretch of the imagination, upset me. "Why would someone think it's a good idea to mark a trail way out here, if that even were their intent?!"

"Whaddaya mean, Josiah" she asked, slinging her backpack to the ground and reaching for her water bottle. She took several sips before handing me the bottle.

"Well, we both know how far off the trail we are. There's no path here. Look where I place us on the map. Now, suppose you're an unsuspecting hiker in trouble, find these and other stacked pebbles around here, and start following them. To where? They'll just lead you further astray. We both know these are nothing but 'trail graffiti,' something someone left to say: 'I got here before you!'

"I think the person who built these stacks has an 'edifice complex.' "

See Endnote 5.

"Sam the Ram" (Photo: K. S. Brooks)
Indies Unlimited, September 29, 2018

"Who is it, Sam?"
"I don't know, Shirley! Looks like one of them city folks,
up here to get pictures of the kids and us."

9. Sam the Ram

"**W**ho is it, Sam?"

"I don't know, Shirley! Looks like one of them city folks, up here to get pictures of the kids and us."

"Well, ask if we can have copies."

"Okay.

"Pardon me, miss, might I take a look at some of the photos you've taken?"

"Sorry, friend. The only thing I can show is what I see in my viewfinder. I'm using a professional 35mm film camera."

"You don't say. I haven't seen one of those in a long time, not since those cell phone thingamabobs came along. What type of film are you using?"

"Fujifilm Superia X-TRA CH 400. It's a great high-speed color negative film. Works well for available light and general use. Good sharpness, too."

"Well, I hope it can reproduce the tonal range I see in the display. On the other hand—"

"On the other hand, *what?*!"

"On the other hand, I've seen some *great* work done using Kodak Porta 400. This film is wonderful for the outdoors. And, it also gives you spectacular skin tones plus exceptional color saturation over a wide range of lighting conditions. Still, if you want warmer tones, you might try Kodak Super gold 400, though it's not as sharp as the Porta."

"Wow. Now you're a film connoisseur? How 'bout you just let me make the decisions regarding my film!"

"Well, you don't have to get huffy about it."

[Several seconds pass in silence.]

"So, what type of camera did you say you were using?"

"Preacher Man" (Photo: Pinterest)

This murder scene was particularly tragic.

10. Preacher Man

Byond the cracked sidewalk, and the telephone pole with layers of flyers in a rainbow of colors, and the patch of dry brown grass there stood a ten-foot high concrete block wall, caked with dozens of coats of paint. There was a small shrine at the foot of it, with burnt out candles and dead flowers and a few soggy teddy bears. One word of graffiti filled the wall, red letters on a gold background: Rejoice![4]

Rejoice, indeed! thought Thaddeus Washington. *Rejoice about wha'? Tha' two people was shot dead in cold blood here two nights ago?!* Minutes earlier, Thaddeus had sat on the steps of the church across the street from the ersatz shrine, which now was deteriorating in the heat and humidity of a Philadelphia summer's day. The shrine was but one of many that had sprung up across the inner city in the last several months.

This murder scene was particularly tragic. It marked a drive-by shooting intended to kill the man sitting on the porch of the dilapidated row house adjacent to the concrete block wall, a wall erected only three months earlier to enclose the burned-out shell of the row house on the corner. The killers succeeded. At the same time, however, several rounds from what observers thought was an AK-47 penetrated the clapboard exterior of the house, killing six-year-old Shanice Causey as she slept on a couch under the front room window. Her death was ruled a homicide—Number 172 in the city this year already. The Philadelphia was well on its way to setting a new homicide

---

[4] This story was entered into the 2018 Owl Canyon Press Hackathon #2 of December, 2018. Here, the sponsors provided the first and 25th paragraphs (**bolded**), and participants were required to provide the 2nd through 24th, and 26th through 50th paragraphs. Each paragraph was required to have at least 40 words.

record! Worse, expectations were that almost half of these killings never would be solved.

Now 80, Thaddeus was the pastor of the church, known formally as the First Liberty Baptist Church. Its roots went back to the time when his father, Josiah, arrived in the city, shortly after the outbreak of World War II. Josiah was a self-taught man of the cloth who, in the early part of the 20th century, had sharecropped in Choctaw County, Alabama. His most important crops were cotton and tobacco. "Always need some 'baccy," the elder Washington used to say at planting time.

Thaddeus was the youngest of six children; others included his brother Bobby, the eldest, and four sisters. Their sharecropper home, if it could even be called that, was a one-room wood shack elevated on cinder blocks. To this day, if you asked him, Thaddeus still called Alabama "home."

Why? Because, he'd tell you as you got to know him, Bobby made the mistake back in '39, just after he, Thaddeus, was born, of saying something—to this day, Thaddeus hasn't a clue what it was—to a white gal as she went into the general store in Butler. The next morning, Josiah found him hanging from a tree by Ulmer Creek.

After Josiah cut him down and buried him, Thaddeus would tell you without emotion (as if he were discussing the weather or what he'd eaten for lunch), his Daddy packed up the family and set out with their mule Daisy and their wagon for the Big Muddy. Just like *that*, Thaddeus would say, snapping his fingers and pursing his lips. "Why hang aroun'?" he'd ask, rhetorically. "Who'd the Klan come for next? Daddy? Mama? One of my sisters?

"Once we got to the river, we took a boat to northern Arkansas—to Osceola," he'd tell you. "Daddy done heard there was good jobs to be had there, an' there was. He got one as a laborer at the Knight Flour Company. Tha' Mr. Knight, he was some kinda rich; he also own' the local radio station: KKFC-AM. So, we stayed. But no, siree, this ain't my home," he'd mutter to himself if you asked him. "Never will be. Not even after all these years. *Alabama* is my home—tha's where Bobby's buried."

"Osceola's sure a long way from Philadelphia," I remarked one day a few weeks earlier as we were sitting on the steps of the church late one Sunday morning following services, taking in the quietude. He nodded, mumbling something about its being more than a thousand miles or so between the two, he guessed. So, I had to ask: "How'd you end up here? Seems a bit strange, when you think about it: sharecropper/preacher man to flour mill laborer . . . and then, your Daddy up and moves the whole clan again, but this time, to The Big City: Phil-a-del-phia! Man, that's a whole world of change."

He nodded as he pulled a weed from a crack in the concrete step beneath his shoes. "You gotta un'erstand," he said, "life down there wasn't much better than what we lef' behind in Alabama. You wanna go to the movies? 'Awright,' says The Man, 'you people just hustle yourselves aroun' to the back of the theater, climb the stairs, and watch from the balcony. Be quiet, y'all hear! And for sure, don't be usin' the same bathrooms we be usin' or drinkin' from the same water fountain. An' hey! We don't wanna see you sittin' at the lunch counters in Walker's Pharmacy on Main Street, either! Best y'all jus' stay on your side of the tracks, and we'll get along fine!' That was life in Osceola!" he spat as he shifted his body on the hot concrete.

"Then, Worl' War II broke out," he continued. "At some point, Daddy receive' a letter from his cousin, who was workin' in the Navy Yard up here. He said they needed people, real bad like, so we packed up again—this time in an ol' 1932 Ford sedan, took US Route 61, the Blues Highway, north out o' town, an' headed for the East Coast. Thank the Lord we had the Green Book to help us fin' places to stay. The whole trip took two weeks, but we finally made it. Rented—and finally purchased—the house next door to where we're sittin'. Been here ever since. In fac', two o' my sisters—Edmonia and Chakaia Washington, both spinsters—live with me to this day. They sing in the church choir.

"Neighborhood's done changed a lot, though, since Daddy preached the gospel, tha's for sure. It was mixed when we firs' rented here . . . lots of Italians, all workin' in the Yard like Daddy. Trees lined the streets then, an' people planted flowers around them . . . zinnias, mostly, an' geraniums, too. But slowly, the whites move' out, especially after the transit strike in 1944, when the PTC wanted to allow black employees to be motormen an' conductors. The straw tha' really broke the camel's back, though, was when Mr. Roosevelt threatened to take over the transit company an' cancel the deferments o' any strikers between 18 and 37. Boy howdy, did the neighborhood empty o' white folks after tha'! An' the res' of us, not having all the money in the worl', jus' watched things go downhill from there. We tried to keep the neighborhood up, but wha' with people startin' to have children an' all, well, you know wha' happens then.

"Not tha' we didn't have a little more money in our pockets than we would've, had we stayed in Osceola. No, siree. Them war years an' the years tha' followed was pretty good, if I say so myself," he continued. "Though 'is health was gettin' bad—I think it had somethin' to do with the dust in the air at the Navy Yard, can't be sure—Daddy started to preach in the old IGA store on the corner nex' to our house on Sunday mornin's . . . where we're sittin' now. The building became the First Liberty Baptist Church when the ol' grocer died. Us neighbors got together an' purchased the property.

"So, between 'is earnin's as a preacher man an' the odd jobs 'e did for others—Daddy was proficient as a plumber an' a handyman—we made out right proper like, enough to get us a new Kaiser-Frazer sometime in the early '50s. I sure loved tha' car! As I recall, it was robin egg blue. An' the new-car smell! Wowie, tha' was unlike anything I ever experienced. Daddy use' to take the whole family for drives on Sunday afternoons. We'd go all over the City, even up the Main Line to see the big homes. Mama say she had to pinch 'erself because it all seemed like a dream."

He wiped the sweat from his forehead with a handkerchief. "Used to be able to sit out on your porch at night," he recalled wistfully, "listen to the ball game or a little music on the staticky radio, talk to your neighbors, enjoy a beer or two, an' jus' kick back after a day's work. Sure, Friday nights would get a little rowdy now an' then, 'specially after a high school football game. But even then, it was mos'ly jus' a few cars full o' kids with the radio turned up too loud, drunken screams from one or two boys who'd had a few too many beers, or some trash thrown onto the street. Nothin' like what you see these days.

"But now, you're takin' your life in your hands if you come outside after dark. An' even when you're inside, bes' to stay in the back o' the house, neares' the alley, or you could end up like them," he warned, jerking his head toward where Shanice Causey and the man on the porch had recently been murdered.

"So, how'd it get to this point, Pastor? I mean, how'd we get to where we are today?" I asked. He turned toward me and shook his head. "It started with the war . . . the Vietnam War, y'know. Tha's what took us down this dark road. I was there. Enlisted in the Army right out o' high school in the summer o' '56, and put in 20 years. First Infantry Division, The Big Red One, *The*

Bloody First. Was at the Battle of Ong Thanh, I was. We took heavy casualties there. An' I fought in the Tet Offensive and in Operation Quyet Thang, too. The boys in the Pentagon called the last one *Resolve to Win.* And then we los' our division commander in Operation Toan Thang. The whole war was a fraud per-per-perpetrated on the American People, an' the government knew it from Day One. I'll never forget being spit on when I got back the West Coast. At least the GI Bill allowed me to get my degree from divinity school.

"Then, of course, there was the assassination o' Dr. Martin Luther King an' Robert Kennedy. Yes, President Johnson moved quickly to put in place his Great Society, an' yes, there was some improvement in our lot over the years. But frankly, despite everythin' tha's been done, the inner cities have turn' into ghettos, with gangs, guns, an' drug-fueled violence dominatin' our people's days an' nights. An' the news? Ever' day it's the same. I don' un'erstand why the local TV stations simply don' televise las' week's crime stories an' cut in today's weather. Won' make no difference 'cept in the body coun'. Another drive-by shootin', another innocent person caught in the crossfire, another hit-and-run, another drug bus' . . . day after day, it's all the same, jus' the names an' the numbers of homicides change."

"So," I said, rising from the steps, which by now had started to heat up in the noonday sun, "who *was* the man on the porch . . . the one the shooter wanted to kill? You must have known him. After all, he apparently lived across the street from you."

"Oh, yes, I knew 'im," said Thaddeus, rising and dusting off the back of his pants with both hands. "Knew 'im well. His name was Jalaal Causey. It was 'is six-year-old sister who was kill' while she slep' in the living room. They live' wi' their grandma, Kareen Parker. God only knows where their father is; 'e took off before Shanice was born. As for their mother, Lysha, she'd been on drugs for the longest time. In fac', Shanice was born with an addiction. It was months before she was releas' from the hospital. After Lysha got out of rehab, some six months after Shanice was born, she disappeared, leaving her 50-year-old mother to care for 'er children. Some said she lef' the city; gone to Atlanta, someone said. Another mentioned Baltimore."

"Wow, no wonder trouble followed them over there, with a family background like that," I said. I had no sooner uttered those words when

Thaddeus abruptly put up his right hand and stopped me. "Whoa, whoa, my frien', you got it all wrong. Those were two o' the fines' kids you could ever hope to meet. Anywhere. Period.

"Jalaal'd been a choir boy since 'e was six. In fac', 'e was still in the choir at the time o' 'is death. He loved the Lord. I confirmed 'im. He always did well in school . . . had a real aptitude for science an' math, tha' boy did. After graduation from high school, 'e attended trade school an' became an electrician. It wasn't eight months ago 'e showed me 'is journeyman electrician an' union papers. He was makin' good coin, too, an' had a bright future. Despite everythin' you see here, 'e had escaped the gangs, drugs, an' violence. He 'ad 'is sights on movin' 'is grandmother an' sister out o' this area, to a place where they would be safer.

"Which is why none o' this makes any sense," the pastor went on, shaking his head. "Why would anyone want to kill Jalaal? Was it simply a deadly case o' mistaken identity? Had Jalaal said somethin' to someone on the street an' they took offense? That wouldn't've been like 'im. He didn't drive, so it wasn't a case o' road rage . . . you know, where someone followed 'im home and shot 'im out o' anger. It jus' doesn't make sense."

Traffic was picking up now as residents drove by on their way to the market, theater, and other weekend destinations. The chalk marks on the street, which showed where shell casings had dropped, already faint, now were being worn away ever more quickly by the tires of passing cars. Soon, like the lives of Jalaal and Shanice Causey, they would disappear forever.

Three days later an automobile pulled up and parked beside the concrete wall. The driver opened the door, but did not get out of the car. Although her face was in shadow, it was easy to tell she was sad. There was something about how she turned away from the sun and rested the weight of her hands on the steering wheel, something about her silent composure, that caused Hannah to sigh. The young girl watched the driver lean out of the car and stretch her hand out towards one of the burned-out candles.

Hannah approached the car and asked the visitor, "Are you thad, mith?" The six-year-old, who spoke with a heavy lisp, was a former playmate of Shanice's. The fact was, the two girls had been inseparable since birth. Not only were they the same age, they were next-door neighbors as well. Now, Hannah was standing next to the shrine, hula hoop in hand.

Hannah was too young to know that the stranger who had stopped was Shanice's mother. But she did understand the impact the shrine had on the visitor. It was one with which Hannah was all too familiar, one she had seen for days after the shooting as neighbors and strangers alike flocked to the corner where the shooting took place, bringing teddy bears, flowers, and other mementos to mark the spot where her dearest friend and her friend's brother had been murdered. There, the tears flowed freely well into the night. There, people stood with candles and recited passages from the Bible, survivors of a tragedy who were helpless to stop the violence, much less bring back the children. No, Hannah understood all too well what must have been going through the stranger's mind.

The driver turned her gaze toward Hannah, nodded, and, brushing aside her tears, closed her door, restarted the engine, and slowly drove away. Hannah waved *bye bye*, a sad look overtaking her face. Her mother, Jazmin Taylor, peered between the curtains from her front room window. Given the shooting, there wasn't a mother on the block who wasn't watching her children—and every other child on the block—throughout the day. She recognized Lysha, and even before the woman's car was out of sight, ran down the steps and grabbed her daughter by the arm.

"What that woman say to you, chil'?!" she demanded of Hannah. "What she want? That woman's no good, chil'. She have no right comin' here like that. What she say to you?!" The answer, of course, and what Hannah told her, was: "She said nuffin', Mama. She jus' sat there and cried."

"She should cry," Mrs. Taylor responded angrily. "Maybe if she'd stayed home and taken care o' her children, this never would've happened. Now, you come in the house this minute, you hear, chil'? I don' want you out here if that woman is maybe comin' aroun' an' talkin' to you!"

Two weeks passed. By now, the shrine—if it even could be called that anymore—had all but disappeared. The teddy bears had disintegrated, and the little vases that once held beautiful cut flowers had been either stolen or smashed by neighborhood vandals. Only the word Rejoice!—painted on the wall—remained to remind people of the incident that took two lives.

Then, there she was again: Lysha Causey. She stopped her car in the same place as before, paused, appeared to be saying something—perhaps a prayer—and finally, after crossing herself, drove away. *Well,* thought Jazmin, *at least we know she's back in town. God only knows where she's staying . . . or with who.*

At church the next Sunday, following the sermon and closing prayer, Jazmin stayed behind to confide in Pastor Washington what she had observed regarding Lysha Causey's two visits to the shrine. "Are you sure it was 'er?" Thaddeus asked inquisitively.

"Oh, yes, Pastor," she assured him, "there isn't a chance it could be someone else. Hannah said she looked sad. When I saw her this week, she seemed to be mumbling a prayer to herself before she made the sign of the cross and drove off. Yes, I'm positive it was her."

Thaddeus put his hand over his mouth and stroked his chin. "Hmmm," he murmured softly, "it makes sense, in a way. A mother grievin'. That's not the order of things. We expect our children to bury *us.* Whatever happened to 'er in the past, it must be terrible to lose a chil', not to mention two. An' in such a terrible way, too. She may've abandon' 'er children, but it's not for us to judge 'er. Remember Chapter 7, Verse 1 of Saint Matthew's Gospel: 'Do not judge, or you too will be judged. For in the same way you judge others, you will be judged, an' with the measure you use, it will be measured to you.'

"We must watch for 'er, sister Jazmin, so, if she's a willin', I kin sit with 'er an' help her through this difficul' time. I'm not always standin' at the front o' my home or sittin' on the steps o' the church. So, if you should see her again—an' I 'spect you *will*—please, *please,* ask 'er to come an' talk with me."

The two parted, pleased in a way that somehow, something good still might come from what had been the most heart-wrenching tragedy the neighborhood ever had experienced. To make matters worse, the murders of Lysha Causey's children came on top of the highest crime rate and number of shootings the city ever had experienced at this point in a year.

True to Thaddeus's premonition, it was only a matter of weeks before Lysha Causey returned, this time at sunset, late on a Saturday, after it had rained most of the day. The clouds had no sooner parted, however, revealing a glorious red ball of fire, than Lysha pulled her car to the curb in front of the concrete wall and parked.

Hurrying down her front steps, Jazmin Taylor hastily rounded the front of Lysha's car and knocked on the driver's side window. "Lysha, Lysha! It's me, Jazmin. Do you remember me? It's been six years, Lysha!" she shouted, trying to make herself heard through the closed window. "Open the window! Please. Talk to me."

Lysha appeared embarrassed. After all, it had been years since the two had seen each other, And what was she to say? What *could* she say?! *Gee, it's great to see you, Jazmin. Sorry I ran off without saying goodbye, leaving my mother to raise my children, but I just didn't want to deal with the family anymore.* How would that sound?

The fact was, she *couldn't* deal with her family anymore. Her cocaine addiction had reached epic proportions—so great, in fact, she would have sold her soul to the Devil for a fix. By the time her daughter had been born, she had sold almost everything she owned—including herself.

After abandoning her children, she was picked up by a pimp and taken to Baltimore. It was years before she finally hit rock bottom and was forced into rehab. It didn't "take" on the first try, nor on the second. But three times was the charm, and once out, and having been clean for almost six months, she vowed to return to Philadelphia and seek a new start. That's when she got the news about her children's deaths.

Jazmin heard the sound of the car door unlock. In a second, the two women were in each other's arms, hugging and sobbing. Lysha could not control herself. Her body heaved with emotion as she finally, *finally,* accepted the fact that she never would see her children again, that they now were in the hands of the Lord, and that her having abandoned them to their fate was something for which she could never forgive herself.

They soon were joined by Lysha's mother, Kareen Parker, who threw her hands into the air and, looking skyward, shouted, "Rejoice in the Lord always. My daughter has returned. Again, I say, Rejoice." The three hugged and wept for what seemed minutes before impatient drivers, horns blaring, forced them from the middle of the street onto the sidewalk. Hannah, taken in by the emotion of it all, hugged her grandmother's legs, more out of confusion than empathy for their long-lost neighbor.

The noise from the street drew Thaddeus to his front room window. Seeing the three women and Hannah, he hastily ran out his front door, and, mindful of traffic, beat a path to their side. "Lysha, chil'!" he shouted, throwing his arms out and embracing the woman, who again burst into tears. "Oh, Pastor Washington, what have I done?!" she wailed. Her self-loathing knew no bounds.

Thaddeus held her close as she sobbed. Her body began shaking uncontrollably. Then, she collapsed in his arms. Letting her down slowly, the two ended up sitting side-by-side among the remains of the shrine, Lysha's body broken both in spirit and in form. Jazmin and her mother sat beside them while Hannah hid behind her grandmother, bewildered by what was happening.

Thaddeus, of course, knew he was witnessing but the first stage of Lysha's "confession": the beginning of a process that would entail her overcoming her embarrassment, ignoring what other people thought, admitting what she had done, and confessing her sins to God. Then, and only then, could the healing begin.

"Come with me, sister Lysha. Let us go into the sanctuary across the street an' sit an' talk." He stood, offered his hand, and, helping her to her feet, led the way to his church. "You know, my chil," he continued solemnly, "we can go directly to God anytime and anywhere. He has the power to forgive our sins. As it is said in Luke, Chapter 5, Verse 20: 'Man, thy sins are forgiven thee.'"

Lysha stopped crying. Her demeaner brightened. She smoothed her hair and walked up the church steps with determination. Thaddeus held the door for her and followed her into the sanctuary. There, near the foot of the altar, they talked—and prayed—well into the evening.

It was later that night—much later, at 10:20 p.m., to be exact—that Thaddeus finally was able to take off his shoes, sit back in his recliner, and watch the local news on his television set: *"...and this just in to the Channel 11 Newsroom: moments ago, Philadelphia Police announced the arrest of DeShawn Causey for the murder of Terrell Clarke. Causey, a known drug distributor and gun dealer who had numerous outstanding warrants, had long evaded capture by local, state, and federal authorities. In an unusual twist in this case, an AK-47 found in Clarke's car was traced using shell casings to the murders in the inner city several weeks ago of Causey's son and daughter. Authorities surmise Clarke may have targeted Causey's son, Jalaal, out of anger over a drug deal gone bad. Causey's daughter, Shanice, apparently was in the wrong place at the wrong time.* [News anchor sets aside the Breaking News bulletin and turns to the station's meteorologist.] *Well, Valarie, I guess we at least can rejoice in the fact the police have solved these two murders!* [Pause.] *So, moving ahead to the weather, whaddaya have in store for us in the days ahead?"*

"Road to Autumn" (Photo: K.S. Brooks.)
Indies Unlimited, October 7, 2018

**"I was on the road one night, driving through the
California desert, and heard the Kingston Trio track."**

11. Road to Autumn

"**Hi-** yah, Frankie!"

"Hey, kid. What brings ya to Patsy's?"

"You said they had the best food in town, so I thought I'd give it a try. What a surprise to find *you* here!"

"Have a seat, my friend. Hey, Salvatore. Salvatore! My friend just joined me. How 'bout a menu?

"So, what's up?"

"Not much. But this does give me a chance to ask a question that's been on my mind for some time."

"Shoot!"

"That song you debuted on the celebration of your 50th birthday: *It Was A Very Good Year.* You know, the one with the lyrics, 'But now the days are short, I'm in the autumn of my years . . . .' "

"Whoa, hold on, kid." Sinatra started to laugh. "I didn't debut that song. Ervin Drake wrote that piece back in 1961, when he was in a bit of a slump. Fact is, he hadn't had a hit in eight years. So, he's talking with an old pal one morning, sits down at the piano, and finishes the whole thing in ten minutes. I'm not kidding."

[Salvatore brings the menu.] "Thanks, pal.

"Anyway," Sinatra continues, "the Kingston Trio recorded the piece that year, though the song—and the album it was in—went nowhere."

"So, how'd *you* pick it up?"

"I was on the road one night, driving through the California desert, and heard the Kingston Trio track. I knew immediately: this was the song!

"Never underestimate the power of serendipity, kid!"

"Anthony" (Photo: K. S. Brooks)
Indies Unlimited, October 13, 2018

Jeff and I had been watching a lone hawk circling
a farmer's field at 100 feet in the early evening sky.

12. Anthony

Y ou look deep in thought."

"Huh? Oh, sorry. I was thinking about Anthony Bourdain?"

"Anthony Bourdain?! What in the world brought *him* to mind?"

Jeff and I had been watching a lone hawk circling a farmer's field at 100 feet in the early evening sky. Spotting an errant field mouse that dared to emerge from his nest, the raptor dove, snatched the poor creature with her talons, and after flying to feed her chicks in a nearby tree, returned to her vigil in the sky.

"In a way, Tony was a lot like that hawk," I said, shifting my position on the ground to steady myself as I aimed my camera upward. "I've watched his show since it first came on the air. Think about it. Tony was passionate . . . about life in general and his pursuits in particular; focused . . . not on materialistic things but on the truths that he drew from his travels; and above all, free . . . free from outside pressures to do what *he* wanted to do."

"So, for a man who seemed to have it all, how would you explain his death?"

"Well, at heart, Tony always struck me as a very private person. A loner. A man who kept his own counsel. And that can be a sad, depressing existence."

53

"Secret of the Cave" (Photo: K. S. Brooks)
Indies Unlimited, October 20, 2018

"Well, we made it. What's it been?
Sixty years the four of us 've been coming here?"

13. Secret of the Cave

"**W**ell, we made it. What's it been? Sixty years the four of us've been coming here?" announced Greg, trying to catch his breath. He set his bottle carrier on the cave floor.

Ed nodded. "Well, until the early '70s, it was five . . . you, Charlie, Bill, Jeff, and me. Talk about an unholy collection of misfits!"

"I know," agreed Bill, using his cuff to wipe his brow, "though I have to say, I long suspected Charlie and Maria snuck up here more than a few times after school for a little fun, if you catch my drift."

Charlie threw a punch at him in the air. "Hey! I thought that was our secret! I'm telling her what you said when I get home. She'll clean your clock the next time she sees you!"

Greg lifted the Champagne from its carrier, popped the cork, and, after withdrawing several plastic cups from his knapsack, poured four servings. "Here's to Jeff," he intoned, "the best friend a guy could have."

They touched cups and emptied them, whereupon Greg filled them again. "Remember how crazy Jeff always was in school, how Sister Theresa was always watching him out of the corner of her eye, tapping her ruler on her hand, and then, WHACK! She'd hit him on the wrist. Not once, but three times. And he never cried."

"I know," replied Bill, downing his second cup. "He was a good kid. He didn't deserve to die in Nam."

"Jack is Back" (Photo: K. S. Brooks)
Indies Unlimited, October 27, 2018

Martelli looked to his right, where the visage of a devilish face, this one celebrating the day when ghosts and witches are said to appear, seeming smiled at him.

14. Jack is Back

"Waddaya got for me, Michael?" asked Detective Lou Martelli, NYPD, as he stepped into the garden of a townhouse in the West Village early in the evening on Halloween, 2017.

"The usual," deadpanned Deputy Coroner Michael Antonetti. He pulled a white sheet over the victim, closed his medical bag, stood, and faced the detective. "White male, about 40 years of age, medium build, sliced and diced like that jack-o'-lantern grinnin' at you from over there."

Martelli looked to his right, where the visage of a devilish face, this one celebrating the day when ghosts and witches are said to appear, seeming smiled at him. "Well, he sure looks like he knows something but ain't talkin'," replied Martelli, taking out his notebook. "So, any murder weapon?"

"Oh, yeah, we got a murder weapon, all right," nodded the coroner, handing Martelli a sealed, tagged evidence bag. "Even better than that, we got the whole kit and caboodle; we got ourselves an entire set of murder weapons."

"Whaddaya mean, Michael?"

"What I mean is, we got ourselves a complete set of pumpkin carving sculpting tools. Whoever killed our John Doe, here, musta interrupted the guy while he was working on his pumpkin because the vic's stomach looks like ol' jack's."

"Well, it just confirms what we already know," replied Martelli.

"What's that?"

"Pumpkin carving is one of the most dangerous things a person can do! Don't you remember? There're almost 2000 pumpkin carving injuries nationwide every year during October and November."[5]

---

[5] Det. Louis Martelli, NYPD, is the protagonist in six murder mystery/thrillers penned by the author, all of which are based on real life or on stories ripped from the headlines: https://www.amazon.com/gp/product/B07HRFJ8FT/ref=series_rw_dp_sw
Audiobooks also are available for the series on Amazon's *Audible* platform.

"Last Train Home" (Photo: Photographer Unknown)
Peter C. Cobeen, Train Engineer, 1861 - 1952
http://iagenweb.org/history/IAfamilies/CobeenFamily.htm

It sounds like dad's hand on the whistle cord more than 40 years ago,
thought John; *that same mournful sound, that same wail in the night.*

15. Last Train Home

It must have been the way the engineer stepped on the sequencer pedal to sound the diesel's horn that caught John Lambert's attention—two long, one short, and one *extra*-long burst of compressed air—as the three locomotives, operating in tandem and pulling more than two hundred freight cars, sped through the remote, unprotected railroad crossing on a moonless, rainy night in central Illinois. *It sounds like dad's hand on the whistle cord more than 40 years ago,* thought John; *that same mournful sound, that same wail in the night.* It used to be his father Tony's way of letting the family know he was coming home from the north-end of a run as he neared the Beacon Hill switch.

The boxcars flashing before his eyes took John back to his childhood, a time when he and his father would drive this road every Saturday morning on their way south out of town to the farmer's market. Now, John was headed home after spending an evening chatting over beers with a childhood friend who lived in John's old home town.

That's a long rattler, he thought, listening to the clickety-clack sounds of the steel wheels as they crossed the open joints in the rails. Though the train was streaking by at more than 40 miles-per-hour and the rain—smeared by his worn wiper blades—blurred his vision, he still could make out several railroad reporting marks and emblems on the sides of the boxcars illuminated by his vehicle's headlights. Represented were such fallen flags as B&O: Baltimore and Ohio; IC: Illinois Central; and LV: Lehigh Valley. His father had known all of the railroad "abbreviations." He, John . . . well, truth be told, he knew *almost* all of them. It was a game they had played: Name That Railroad.

Let's see, he thought: *FGER: Fruit Growers Express Company; IN: Illinois Northern; ATSF: Atchison Topeka & Santa Fe.* He began singing to himself: *Folks around these parts get the time of day, From the Atchison, Topeka and the Santa Fe.*[6] John laughed. *Bing Crosby I'm not.* He continued scanning the sides of the boxcars. *ESLJ. ESLJ? What the heck is that?!*

What's the matter, John? asked the ghost voice in the passenger seat to his right. *Don'tcha know that one?* The voice let out a deep belly laugh, more out of love than anything else. Still, the gauntlet had been thrown down. "I'm sure I know what it is," John muttered, as if his father were sitting beside him. *Of course you do, Son. Here, I'll give ya a hint: the first letter stands for East.*

John could hear his father laughing—laughter that slowly dissolved into the clatter of the last few boxcars as they disappeared to John's left, leaving only the flashing rear end light on the last car visible for a few seconds before it, too, faded into the darkness.

John shifted his car into DRIVE and proceeded slowly over the poorly maintained crossing. He shook his head in disbelief. *Has it really been 40 years since the accident?* he thought. Sadly, it had been . . . almost 40 years to the day since the accident on the Main Line that killed his father and changed John's life forever. *And to think,* he remembered, *it was only days before his parents' 12th wedding anniversary.*

John grew up around the red brick passenger station and wooden freight house near the family home on Piedmont Avenue. Tony often let him ride in the locomotive cab with him when he was in the switchyard. Today, it took but the slightest whiff from a fire—produced, perhaps, by someone burning leaves—to trigger memories of the sulfuric odor of smoke from those old, coal-burning, fire-breathing steam engines, coal smoke that drifted across Piedmont Avenue and brought with it the fine particles of black soot that invaded every aspect of the Lamberts' home and lives.

Depending on the weather—mostly on the wind—the soot could be found everywhere: in their nostrils, their mouths, and their hair. They slept with it; watched it cover their tables, chairs, and cabinets; and saw curtains go from white to gray within a week. Even Tony's nightly bath couldn't remove the coal dust from his tired, spent body. The railroad, in fact, was slowly penetrating every aspect of his life, *of his very being.* And though he couldn't have known it, it wouldn't be long before his employer, the Chicago,

---

[6] On The Atchison, Topeka And The Santa Fe lyrics © Sony/ATV Music Publishing LLC; Songwriters: Harry Warren/Johnny Mercer

Springfield, and Western Railroad—the CSW—soon would lay claim to his life.

ESLJ? ESLJ? What could that be?!

That fateful night in October, 1948, the night of the accident, was moonless, with rain. Tony wasn't even supposed to have been working. He'd already put in his time for the week, taking several trains to both the south and north ends of the line's system each day. But an urgent telephone call from the station master on Piedmont Avenue called him back to the yard after dinner. A major customer in Chicago needed delivery by the next morning, and there was no one available to take a special run into the city. Of course he would do it, said Tony. *Of course he would,* thought John. *My dad was their go-to guy, the man who never said "no." Of course he would take the train to Chicago.*

It was a story that had played out a thousand times in his mind since that night, when he was ten years old. There wasn't a day he *didn't* think about it. His mother already knew, when she heard her husband on the phone, what was about to happen. Even before Tony hung the telephone handset on the hook, she had made and wrapped two salami sandwiches, then poured what remained in the coffee pot on the stove into a Thermos mug, all of which she snugged into his lunch bucket. A quick kiss and he was gone. Nothing unusual there. They'd done it myriad times, day in and day out, as ordinary an activity as you might have seen in any working-class home on the block.

According to the local yard dispatcher, the run into Chicago should have been routine and, indeed, it was. Tony's train comprised five boxcars and a caboose, the five cars loaded with parts that, once assembled, would be shipped to an automobile manufacturer in Detroit. That portion of the run went well. However, problems with the packing around several of his engine's drive-wheel bearings delayed Tony's return home until the early hours of the following day.

As he headed southbound out of Chicago, Tony was aware that speeding toward him—*on the same track*—was another CSW train northbound for Chicago. That one, a consist, was the scheduled early morning run comprising a baggage car and four passenger cars. However, he had been assured, prior to leaving Chicago, that the departure of the northbound passenger train from Springfield to Chicago would be delayed to ensure both trains' safety.

"Now, don't ya worry, Tony. We're doin' maintenance on the northbound track outta Lexington north to Pontiac. You'll have plenty o' time to make it safely to the siding after the Pontiac switch before ya meet that northbound train on the southbound tracks. I got everythin' set up fer ya with the dispatcher in Springfield," the dispatcher in Chicago assured him as Tony departed the Windy City.

Alas, it wasn't to be. Whether someone failed to follow orders or missed a signal never was determined. What is known, though, is that Tony's train had barely gotten up to speed after taking on water in Pontiac before he must have been startled to see the headlight of the oncoming locomotive driving toward him—head-on!—through the rain. By then, it would have been too late for either engineer to act.

People in the area reported hearing a thunderous crash followed immediately by the sounds of two engine boilers exploding. The passenger cars were so mangled, and the people in them so severely injured, that it was impossible for anyone to do anything for them until emergency personnel and wreckers arrived. Tony and his fireman died instantly, as did the engineer and fireman of the northbound passenger train. Not one of their bodies was recovered. Of the passengers, the 15 who died were in the first car behind the baggage car. An additional 43 passengers and the conductor on the passenger train suffered various injuries, ranging from fractures to minor burns.

Today, John can recall the events that followed the accident as if they happened yesterday. Over a beer—okay, maybe two or three—and especially if it's raining and the sky is moonless, he might tell you about the mass held for his dad at St. Michael's Catholic Church a few days after the accident, just as he told his childhood friend, Darin Coopersmith, when they met earlier this evening at a small bar not far from the switchyard where John's dad used to work.

"It began at ten in the morning and lasted more than an hour," John intoned, finishing off his first beer and signaling for a second. "In the absence of my dad's body, a covered catafalque—I hope I pronounced that right—was used to represent his casket. The decorated bier rested in state during the funeral. It was surrounded by three candles on each side. Our local Roman Catholic priest, Father Sutton, officiated.

"I especially remember my mom. She was, like, in total shock. All the color was drained from her face. She wasn't even crying. I don't think she had any tears left. She just sat there, rocking side to side with her eyes closed, hugging my little four-month-old sister, Joyce, and murmuring 'Oh, God, Oh, God.'

"After the ceremony, everyone was coming up to me and saying things like: 'You're the man of the house now, Johnny,' and 'Your mom's gonna need you more than ever.' 'Yes, sir, I'll do my best,' I answered, but it scared the bejesus outta me, I'll tell you that, Darin. I mean, taking care of mom and my sister, and all. Whew, that was a tall order."

John took out a cigarette, flicked his butane lighter, and lit up. Taking a deep drag, he closed his eyes and slowly released the smoke toward the ceiling. Then he continued.

"Just before we left the church, a man from the union gave my mother an envelope—she said it contained a check. That helped some. Still, within a month, we had to move down-state to live with her sister's family. It was all right, I guess, but I missed you and my other friends . . . and, of course, the old neighborhood."

Darin took a sip of his beer and wiped his lips with his right sleeve. "So, did they ever determine what caused the accident?"

John ashed his cigarette in the porcelain tray on the counter. "Not really. Some old newspaper clippings my mother stashed in the attic—I didn't find them until after she died of lung cancer back in 1980—showed a coroner's jury convened four weeks after the crash found the dispatcher in Springfield guilty of gross negligence and recommended he be prosecuted on multiple charges of fourth-degree manslaughter. In the end, though, all the charges against him were dropped."

"But the railroad certainly must have borne *some* blame," Darin replied. His comment appeared to be tendered more out of sympathy than curiosity.

"Ah, yes, the railroad," John muttered, taking another drag on his cigarette. "They got theirs, all right, but not in the courts. CSW's insurance carrier, noting they were already six months behind in their premium payments, issued a notice of cancellation. Attempts by state regulators and city officials to convince them otherwise failed. In the end, the company's board of directors petitioned the Illinois Public Service Commission for authority to cease service, which was granted. A week later, the railroad made its last run from Chicago to Springfield. Try as it might, the board couldn't find a buyer, and the line was dismantled a year later. Those engines and cars not sold were scrapped. And that was the end of the CSW.

"You know, Darin, when I think about it, what I missed most, and still do to this day, were the times dad and I spent together in the switchyard and in the car on Saturday mornings."

He finished his beer, stubbed out his cigarette in the tray, said goodbye to his friend, and departed. John faced a long ride home. His journey would take him south, out of town, down the road and over the tracks toward the farmer's market. The memories, moonless night, and rain weren't going to make the trip easy.

ESLJ? ESLJ? Oh! I know! It's the East St. Louis Junction, Dad.

I knew you'd eventually get it, Son, replied the ghost passenger in the seat to his right.

"Grand Entrance" (Photo: K. S. Brooks)
Indies Unlimited, November 10, 2018

"This is the grand entrance to one of the two concert halls of the Warsaw National Philharmonic Symphony Orchestra in 1938."

16. Grand Entrance

"Where did you find this picture?"

"In the basement of my grandfather Amadei's luthier shop in Ozone Park, Queens. He had it tucked in the corner of the frame holding a picture of my grandmother, Martyna. They came to the United States after the war with the help of Amadei's brother and began fixing violins as well as giving lessons."

"So, why do you think this picture was so important to him?"

"According to the notation on the back—my mother read it to me—this is the grand entrance to one of the two concert halls of the Warsaw National Philharmonic Symphony Orchestra in 1938. She also told me Amadei and Martyna had met as students while attending the Warsaw Institute of Music in the mid-1930s, both privileged to have been chosen to study the violin under Maestro Mieczyslaw Mosze Fliderbaum, chief violinist for the Warsaw Philharmonic. But their dreams of becoming professional musicians grew dark with the rise of Hitler and the Third Reich. They were finally shattered with the invasion of Poland by the Nazis in September of 1939, and with the couple's confinement to the largest ghetto in all of Europe. In the end, following the revolt of April, 1943, those who survived, including Amadei and Martyna, were deported to Treblinka.

"Apparently, this picture was the only thing he took with him except for the clothes on his back."

See Endnote 6.

"Chauncey" (Photo: Missy Cohen)

"Missy, do you think they'll spot us?"

17. Chauncey

"**M**issy, do you think they'll spot us?"

"Not a chance, Chauncey, not while we're wearing these glasses. They're super disguises."

"I hope so. We've put in a lotta time on this case. I'd hate to think, just as we were closing in on the perps, they'd see us and beat it outta town."

"I know, buddy. Don'tcha worry about that. Think about what's going to happen after the police collar them. Think about the media coverage, all those interviews and appearances on the news shows."

"Do you think they'll let me speak? You know, it's not like everyone lets animals talk."

"We talk, Chauncey. To me, you're just like people."

"I know, Missy, but most people never really *speak* to us intelligently or even let us talk. All we hear is 'Who's a good boy?' and stuff like that. We're never taken seriously."

"That's not true. For example, some writers let dogs play very important roles in their stories."

"Name one."

"Well, how about Sir Arthur Conan Doyle? He wrote a wonderful story, 'The Adventure of Silver Blaze'. Remember that one? It involved the disappearance of a famous racehorse, Silver Blaze, and the murder of its trainer. A dog played the key role in how Sherlock Holmes solved the crime. Didn't you like that story?"

"Oh, yes, I thought that was absolutely terrific. But it would have been a much better story if Conan Doyle had given the dog a speaking part."

See Endnote 7.

"High School Reunion" (Photo: Pinterest)

"Welcome home," I shouted to my wife, Marsha, as she alighted from a rail passenger car at the Trenton train station upon returning from her 30th high school reunion in New York City."

18. High School Reunion

"Welcome home," I shouted to my wife, Marsha, as she alighted from a rail passenger car at the Trenton train station upon returning from her 30th high school reunion in New York City. "So, how'd it go?"

"Oh, it went fine," she responded with an air of finality and a broad smile on her face. "Just fine!" She pecked me on the cheek, handed me her overnight bag, and, after switching her crossbody handbag from her right to her left side, followed me to the parking garage.

Whaddaya know?! I thought. I was surprised. Truth be told, I'd been reluctant to ask, given the circumstances surrounding her trip. I'd watched through the years as first, an invitation for her 10th reunion arrived in the mail, and then, one for her 20th. Both were met with the same pursed lips and scowl. Within a minute, each invitation was torn in half, quartered, and dispatched to the trash. Obviously, my expectations for the half-life of the invitation to her 30th had not been good. Yet here she was, back from the event, mind intact and a smile on her face. Life is full of surprises!

The ride to Washington Crossing, our home since we graduated from college, was spent mostly in silence, punctuated now and then by comments she made regarding the compositions aired on the local classical music station.

"Well, at least it must've been nice to see some of your old classmates after all this time," I finally opined. "I know *I'd* be curious about some of the guys I went to school with, that's for sure."

Silence. We were in different worlds. But she did seem at peace with herself.

It's not as if she never spoke about high school. Occasionally, while we were dating—we met when she was a freshman in college, and I was a sophomore—she would talk about growing up on Manhattan's Upper East Side and attending a private high school located not far from her apartment building on Lexington Avenue. She had a good friend—as I recall, her name was Julie—who lived nearby. I specifically remember they shared the same birth date and were once inseparable. They took all the same classes, double dated, dined and attended the theater with their parents together—things like that. They spent summers at a camp in Maine, too, where they were teammates, counselors-in-training, and then, counselors. They apparently were the kind of kids that, if you didn't know better, you'd think were fraternal twins. And yes, she once mentioned they often completed each other's sentences.

So, I was perplexed when both the 10ᵗʰ and 20ᵗʰ reunions passed without the slightest hint of interest on Marsha's part. *Not even an interest in seeing Julie again?* I thought at the time, not that I brought it up.

Friends come and go. God knows that's the truth. I hadn't seen any of *my* high school classmates since leaving the Midwest 30 years earlier. With the exception of two men, I don't even correspond with any of my former classmates, and those two I met at college. Life moves on—the Army, jobs, kids. High school? That's ancient history.

It's not like she didn't talk about those days, though. Often, on our autumn walks along the Delaware—at the spot where Washington crossed that great river on Christmas Night in 1776—she would recite portions of Helen Hunt Jackson's 'October's Bright Blue Weather' or of Molière's *Don Juan*, both of which she learned in two of her favorite high school classes, English and Drama. The fact is, she *loved* high school, which made her attitude toward class reunions all the more puzzling.

It came as a surprise to me, then, how she responded when the invitation for the 30ᵗʰ reunion arrived. Instead of the expected grimaces and conspicuous destruction of the formal announcement, Marsha promptly sat, completed the enclosed form, made her dinner selection, penned a check, and marched to the mailbox at the end of our driveway, where she deposited the return envelope in the mailbox for the next day's pickup.

"Well, that's a change," I noted, setting aside *The Philadelphia Enquirer* and taking a sip of my coffee. "Frankly, I'm thrilled to see you taking advantage of the opportunity to rekindle some old friendships. I'll bet it'll be fun to see your former classmates and learn what's happened to them over the years, especially in the case of your friend Julie. Gosh, you two were like sisters."

"Julie's dead!" she snapped, nearly biting my head off. "She died two years ago—ovarian cancer. Her mother told my mother at one of their card games. Mom called me."

"I'm sorry, darling."

"Well, I am, too. But it's over. And now, it's time to put the record straight."

Put the record straight? What the hell is she talking about? I said nothing, letting her words hang in the air. If this conversation were to continue, it would have to be on *her* terms. For my part, I had no idea how to defuse the land mine I'd stepped on!

We sat in silence for several seconds before she spoke.

"It started near the end of our senior year, and always on a Monday morning. Julie would arrive late, well after first period, and use the same excuse: she had to either stay home to help her mother—who she said had leukemia—or take her mother for an early morning doctor's appointment. This garnered all kinds of sympathy from the school administrators and teachers who, of course, took her at her word. No one dared contact her parents, fearing a call might bring her terminally ill mother to the phone. We, her classmates, were horrified by the news and gave her all the support and sympathy we could.

"Over time, her tardiness turned into day-long absences, something, she said, had to do with her having to stay at the hospital with her mother while she underwent chemotherapy. Again, all of this was excused by the school without the slightest request for a note from home."

"Did you ask her what type of leukemia she had? There are several types, you know."

Marsha laughed. "You're kidding me, right? I was a high school senior. What did I know about leukemia?!

"Anyway, it didn't take long before I began to suspect her story. It didn't make sense. For one thing, I ate dinner at Julie's several times each month—they lived in the apartment building across the street from ours, you know—and I used to, like, nonchalantly but carefully look at her mother when we were talking at the table. I never once saw *anything* that told me she was ill. Not once! The woman always seemed so vibrant, talking about the latest Broadway play she had seen or an exhibit she had taken in at the Metropolitan Museum of Art. She never uttered a word about being sick or having seen a doctor. Nothing! And besides, she had a full head of hair; beautiful, silky blonde hair that fell well below her shoulders. Chemotherapy, my foot!

"I also told my mother what Julie had said. She was aghast. She couldn't believe it. Aside from a cold Julie's mother had had earlier in the year, mom said the woman was as healthy as a horse. And mom would've known; they were bridge partners, played every week—twice, not counting the tournaments they entered.

"Meanwhile, I guess my skepticism started showing."

"Whaddaya mean?"

"I began to give Julie the cold shoulder. Basically, I began ignoring her."

"And?"

"And, the other girls turned on me; said I was a bitch; told me I had no empathy and wasn't the kind of friend Julie needed now, when her mother was dying."

"That musta been rough."

"They were unbelievably cruel. They excluded me from all their activities just at the time when our senior year was coming to a close. For that, I never forgave them."

"And Julie?"

"Ah, yes . . . dear Julie. The straw that broke the camel's back was the day my mother took me downtown for an early Monday morning appointment to have my teeth cleaned. We no sooner had left the dentist's office when I saw Julie and her college boyfriend hail a cab in front of a hotel on the other side of 3rd Avenue. Now I'm starting to think. What if they'd spent the night there? So much for taking care of her mom on Monday mornings!

"I confronted her later that day between classes and told her what I'd seen. She broke down and admitted it was all a hoax, that there was nothing wrong with her mother! The unmitigated gall of that woman! I was furious!"

The fire in my wife's eyes at that moment was unlike anything I'd ever seen. "Sounds like mental illness to me, perhaps a form of Munchausen syndrome by proxy, except her mother wasn't even aware of the fact her daughter was asserting she had leukemia. Just an extreme attempt to get sympathy and special attention, or—"

"Or what?!" Marsha snapped.

"Or she simply wanted to spend as much time as possible with her boyfriend before he went home for the summer and didn't give a flying fig about anyone or anything else, including you, her best friend."

"You got that right! And because of that, her friends turned the last semester of my senior year into a living Hell! Which is where I told Julie she could go. And that was the end of that.

"Now, the rest of the class will learn the truth about Julie. And if they don't believe me, they can ask her mother, who's not only alive and well, but who still plays a brilliant game of contract bridge twice a week with my mother on the Upper East Side."

"Thanksgiving Table" (Photo: K. S. Brooks)
Indies Unlimited, November 24, 2018

"I see you're expecting company, so we won't stay but a minute."

19. Thanksgiving Table

"I hope we're not intruding, Mildred. Ed and I were driving to Seattle to join our daughter and her family for Thanksgiving dinner when we decided to stop and say 'Hello.' Gosh, what's it been?—ten years since we've seen each other?"

"Patricia, Ed! What a surprise! Come in, come in, it's a nasty out there. We had six inches of new snow last night and the temperature's right at the freezing mark. John left for town a half hour ago to pick up a few things for dinner, but he'll be back shortly."

"Well, we certainly don't want to intrude," Mildred replied, stepping into the house and taking off her boots. She placed them on a rug in the vestibule before stepping into the combination living and dining room.

"What a *beautiful* home you've made for John and yourself. I've been telling Ed for years we need to put LA in the rear-view mirror—the traffic and crowding is really getting to me—and move closer to the grandchildren. But, as usual, he insists on sticking it out as long as he has work."

"I understand that, Patricia."

"Anyway, I see you're expecting company, so we won't stay but a minute. Just wanted to see how you're both doing."

"Oh, we're fine, but we're not having guests. The extra settings are in memory of our two sons. We lost them, you know, in the battle for Fallujah in 2004."

"A Performance Interrupted" (Photo: Alexander Böhm;
public domain)
Joshua Bell in Leipzig (2016)

**"I want to congratulate you on your performance,
what there was of it."**

20. A Performance Interrupted

"Joshua, Joshua!"

"Oh, I didn't see you in the rush to get everyone out of the concert hall."

"Well, there was that, all right. But I want to congratulate you on your performance, what there was of it."

[Bell laughs.] "Well, it's certainly not the easiest composition to perform, that's for sure, especially given those lightning quick passages in the first and third movements."

"I know. It wasn't until three years after the piece was written that Adolf Brodsky was able to premier it."

"I guess Tchaikovsky was taking his disastrous three-week long marriage and suicide attempt out on us poor violinists. What other explanation can there be?"

"Frankly, I don't know how you managed to get as far as you did. I saw you staring at the ceiling constantly. At first, I thought you were simply gazing up there as one does while playing . . . you know, looking here and there, up and down. Then, as time went on, I saw you focus more and more on those old supporting beams dating back to the Academy of Music's birth in 1856. But I never expected you to stop the performance and yell to the maestro to get everyone out of the concert hall.

"My God, man. If you hadn't done that, there's no telling how many lives would've been lost when the ceiling collapsed."[7]

---

[7] Ms. Suzanne Pentz, of Kiest and Hood, Architects and Engineers, discovered a major crack in the supporting beams of the ceiling, roof, and support for the chandelier at the Academy of Music in Philadelphia, Pennsylvania, immediately prior to a performance in 1989. This required the cancellation of a performance shortly after it began and the relocation of the Academy's orchestra until repairs could be made.

"Oak Creek" (Photo: K. S. Brooks)
Indies Unlimited, December 15, 2018

Gray Wolf stood on the bank overlooking the Oak Creek rapids.

21. Oak Creek

Gray Wolf stood on the bank overlooking the Oak Creek rapids as the water rushed toward its convergence with the Verde River to the south. It had taken me several years to find him for a magazine article I was writing and more than a year before he agreed to meet with me.

He was Cherokee by birth. His ancestors had been rounded up and forced to march to Oklahoma in 1839. From there, some eventually moved west, Gray Wolf's among them. Now, we stood together in silence, watching the rapids and listening to the babbling of the fast-flowing water.

He saw me staring at the feather he was holding in his left hand.

"I see you are curious about this feather," he said, breaking the silence. "It was my great grandfather's, Thunder Cloud's. He died on the Trail Where They Cried and was buried in a grave that is unmarked to this day."

"Why do you carry it?" I inquired.

"So that I will forever have a reminder of the brutality inflicted upon my People."

"But isn't the written record adequate for capturing the truth?" I replied, making some notes.

"History can be rewritten," he asserted. "My people only trust memory to keep the sacred flame of truth alive. This feather is to remind me of my People's *true* history."

"The Observer" (Photo: U.S. Military; Wikimedia Commons,
public domain)
View of the defendants in the dock at the International Military Tribunal
trial of war criminals in Nuremberg, Bavaria, Germany, November 22, 1945.

"Name, rank, and serial number," barked the MP.

22. The Observer

"**N**ame, rank, and serial number," barked the MP.

"Stan Jacobson, Sergeant First Class, 02356974."

"That's not what's on your dog tag, Jacobson," sneered the MP, grabbing the chain from around the sergeant's neck. "This tag reads 'Glen Peterson'. It says the man's religion is Protestant. Jacobson sounds more Jewish to me. You got some explaining to do, Sergeant!"

"Yeah, well, that dog tag is my lucky charm; took if off Peterson on Omaha Beach, D-Day, 1944. We were in the 116th Infantry, 29th Division. He went down the minute we hit the beach. I knew if the German's took me alive, they'd kill me on the spot. So, I buried my tag in my sock and wore Peterson's right through the war, right up through the Battle of the Bulge and on the tank I rode into Berlin! Here, I'll show you."

He sat, pulled down his sock, and retrieved his dog tag, which he handed to the MP. "That's the real McCoy, but I'll tell you this: I'll wear Peterson's 'till the day I die! It's what got me through the war!"

The MP looked at the tag. Satisfied with its legitimacy, he asked, "Any weapons?"

"Just two knives and a .45."

"Okay, leave 'em in this basket." Then, the MP pointed to the door that led to a balcony overlooking the Nuremberg courtroom. "You have twenty minutes to watch the proceedings. Keep your mouth shut and both hands on the railing in front of you."

"The Race" (Photo: K. S. Brooks)
Indies Unlimited, December 29, 2018

Junior shouldn't have been driving that day.

23. The Race

Despite his being 26 and a veteran of the track, Sean O'Brian, Jr.—everyone called him "Junior"—shouldn't have been driving yesterday. That's his helmet on the ground at the starting line, a tribute to him and something the judges will cite in their opening remarks before the cars take the track for today's first race. But what's tragic is, it all was so avoidable: yesterday's race, the terrible accident, *the fact Junior even was driving.*

Bad enough the track was wet from a downpour earlier in the morning. That alone should have been enough for the officials to delay the race by a day.

And then, there was Junior's dad, Sean, Sr., the man who *should* have been driving for Team O'Brian. At 55, he had more 35 years of racing experience and was more than capable of handling their car on a wet track. Unfortunately, he was sidelined with a dislocated shoulder.

So, despite having injured his wrist in the paddock the day before the race—something over which the medical team fretted but for which they finally gave him clearance—Junior took the green and yellow flag following the restart of the ninth lap. Battling for the lead, his rear end caught the front of another driver's car, sending Junior's car off the wall and back onto the track into the path of the oncoming pack.

He died instantly, leaving behind a wife and three-year-old daughter.

"Moment of Truth" (Photo: fxquadro; Big Stock Photo)

Elsa added something extra, something intriguing: tattoos.

24. Moment of Truth

It was mid-January, 2019. I had agreed to meet her in Stockholm, more for old times' sake than anything else, given my days as a professional wrestler now were far behind me. Truth be told, it probably would be our last time together.

"Did you have a good flight?" I yelled as Elsa cleared Arlanda Airport's customs and rushed toward me, followed by a porter pushing a cart filled with suitcases. Else's father, Liam, and her 14-year-old son, Thad—both of whom infrequently traveled the wrestling circuit with her—brought up the rear. They had flown from Johannesburg whereas I had arrived two hours earlier from Singapore.

Elsa flung herself into my arms, holding tight for what seemed an eternity. I buried my head in her luxurious blond hair and, with every breath, inhaled her intoxicating scent. A torrent of memories coursed through my brain of the nights we had spent together in Dubai, Tokyo, Rio . . . city after city, month after month, year after year . . . chasing each other around the globe, seeking the adulation of crowds clambering to watch, and, yes, perhaps yearning to emulate, the movement of our muscular bodies as we tangled with opponents in the ring.

But Elsa added something extra, something intriguing: tattoos. They were as exquisite as they were intricate, traditional-style renderings with bold lines, bright colors, and iconic designs that covered her arms and legs in spectacular fashion. Because of them, she was barred from competing in bodybuilding competitions. But that didn't prevent her from focusing on muscle definition, proportion, symmetry, ring presence, and the like. And of course, there was her tan. Magnificent!

She was one of the "bad girls" of the professional wrestling circuit and beautiful beyond comparison. All of which made her the one men lusted after. When "on the town," she dressed in Paris's finest; her clothes not only hid the "tats" but instantly made her the focus of every man's—and woman's—attention. She was, in a word, stunning.

Like many in the business, Elsa never married. She had several lovers, of that I was sure. And although we spent considerable time together, the subject of marriage never came up. It wasn't an option, given our lifestyle.

Yet, despite the precautions she *said* she took over the years, it startled me when, in 2004, she disappeared from the circuit—"indisposed," as she put it—only to confide in me little more than a year later that she had given birth to a son she named Thad. There was no mention of the father. I didn't ask!

Not that she owed me an explanation.

The boy, she wrote, would be raised by her parents, who lived near Stockholm. Money wasn't a problem. Her father, a wealthy, retired industrialist, maintained a large estate north of the city, and she asserted the child would have nothing but the finest in the way of care and an education. And love. Lots of love.

It would be another year before Elsa returned to the wrestling circuit, trim as ever.

And so, we picked up where we had left off, again chasing each other around the globe to various championship matches . . . and again sharing an intimate—but guarded—relationship, primarily to protect her privacy in general and her family situation in particular.

Thad, for his part, was an interesting lad, someone she kept hidden from the public's view until he reached his early teens. Then, under the care of her father, Elsa occasionally brought the boy with her to matches. Regardless of the venue, Thad would sit with his grandfather in a private box high above the ring, where the two could watch Else wrestle without their becoming the intense focus of prying eyes.

Not that Thad actually watched the matches, whether they were his mother's or those of other competitors. Anyone who even chanced to see the boy and his grandfather from their seats high in the grandstand could have discerned instantly that Thad, his face expressionless and his body swaying side to side, was disengaged. Clearly, the boy's mind was elsewhere. That, or he was deep in thought.

The fact is, Thad was born with a congenital brain abnormality that made him a megasavant. Think Laurence Kim Peek, the man who inspired the autistic savant character Raymond Babbitt in the movie *Rain Man*. However, unlike Peek, who had an exceptional memory, Thad's area of expertise lay in the field of mathematics.

To him, there was nothing he liked better than to spend an afternoon playing mind games with a number—*any* number—and, having selected it, exploring the number and its digits in all the various and wonderous permutations of which the human mind—*his mind*—could conceive. Divide the number in half, square the digits, sum the squares, repeat the process, render the resulting number as 1's and 0's, look for relationships and oddities, and so and so forth, *ad infinitum, ad nauseum.* This is what he lived for!

Be assured, by the time he had examined the results from every conceivable combination of such mathematical operations, he would have explored hundreds if not thousands of outcomes to the bases 10 and 2, among others. And then, for whatever reason—perhaps because he saw another number in a newspaper or magazine on the desk in the den or in an advertisement displayed on a television screen—he'd be off to the races on yet another mathematical adventure.

He did these calculations in his head, of course! Thad needed neither pencil and paper nor a computer. Else once told me he never used the PC they had purchased for him some years earlier, abandoning it the day after they set it up in his room. "He said it bored him," she mentioned over dinner one night in Mexico City. "And besides, he complained it took too long to solve quartic polynomials, whatever the hell *those* things are."

"Hi ya, Thad," I shouted to the teen as Elsa and I unwillingly released our grips on each other.

Elsa motioned to the boy, beckoning him to come forward while Liam paid the porter.

Thad, saying nothing, approached. He barely looked up to acknowledge my presence.

"Happy New Year, Thad!" I said enthusiastically, extending my hand. "I'll bet you're glad to see 2018 behind you!"

"Did you know 2018 was a happy year?" the boy asked without the least hint of emotion in his voice. He offered no hand. "It's also *odious* because it has an odd number of ones in its binary expansion, 11111100010."

"I had no idea," I exclaimed, my eyes wide with mock surprise.

"Besides, 2018 is twice 1009—that's a prime number, both forward and backward. That's called an emirp," he continued matter-of-factly.

"A *what?*!" I asked, trying to engage him, while winking at Liam.

"It's 'prime' spelled backwards. Did you know that binary representations of the primes below $N = 100$ all begin and end in 1?"

Elsa came to my rescue. "Oh, honey," she interjected, "I'm sure Mr. Conrad would love to sit down and talk to you about your numbers, but sadly, he'll be the first to tell you he simply doesn't have the background and knowledge you possess, do you, Jeffrey?"

"Your mom's right, Thad. When it came time to hand out brains after I was born, I'm afraid I was standing at the back of the line. But thank God there are people like you, son . . . you know, people who really understand that stuff. Heck, without it, we'd never have made it to the Moon, that's for sure."

Thad continued talking as if he hadn't heard a word his mother or I had said. "And half of 2018—1009—is a happy number, too, because if you take the sum of the squares of its digits—"

"Now, Thad!" his mother admonished.

"And did you know that 2 raised to the 2019th power contains 666, the number of the beast?" he continued, undeterred.

There simply was no stopping his train of thought.

"Thad! Please!" said Elsa, exasperated. "Let's not wear out our welcome. Mr. Conrad was so kind to pick us up at the airport. We certainly wouldn't want to spoil it by bending his ear the entire trip home with talk of mathematics. Tell Mr. Conrad about your flight and the interesting man you sat with. Tell him about the man's dog. What was its name? Let me think. Roffe. Yes, that's it. Roffe. As I recall, he said it was a golden retriever. Remember?"

Thad didn't skip a beat. "The golden ratio is a logarithmic spiral whose growth factor—"

"Thad! Stop it! Just stop it!" Elsa, exhausted, had reached her limit.

Thad sank into his seat on the airport bus as we drove toward the car park. Once the vehicle had come to a stop in back of my rental Mercedes, we hopped out. I opened the Mercedes' trunk, and while Liam stowed their luggage, Elsa settled Thad in the back seat. Wedging my suitcase in last, I slammed the trunk's lid and headed toward the front.

"So, is this really your last 'hurrah?' " I asked, climbing into the sedan as Elsa got in the passenger side. Liam joined Thad in the back.

"Yes, nothing like going out with a bang," Elsa said, smiling. "But it's time to leave the ring. The physical abuse is taking its toll, and I'm not getting any younger, you know. Besides, I want to spend more time with Thad."

It didn't take long to exit the airport and within minutes, we were headed toward Elsa's parents' estate, which was located near Uppsala.

"I've decided this is to be my last match," she stated resolutely. "Fortuitously, it's being held in Stockholm; that way, both of my parents will be able to attend. They're the ones who sacrificed all these years, first by helping me get my career off the ground, and then, by taking care of Thad when I went back on the road. I don't know what I would've done without them."

I nodded but said nothing.

"And there was never a word from them about what I should do or should have done at any time in my life," she continued. "We just played the hand dealt us and went from there. Not even when I came home and told them I was pregnant; not one question, not even 'who is the father?' They musta figured I'd work it out, regardless of whether I wanted the man in my life or in the life of my unborn child.

"And then, when Thad was born and we realized he had abnormalities, they never, *never* questioned me about what I wanted to do. They just rolled up their sleeves and jumped in to help take care of him while I got ready to get back on the road," she said, pulling some stray strands of hair back behind her right ear.

"That must've been tough," I said, "especially in the early years, when he needed extra attention and care."

"Well, it wasn't easy, but he *is* high functioning. He's always washed and dressed himself, even at an early age, and he did as well as could be expected in private school, especially in math, of course." She laughed. "On the other subjects . . . well, not so much. He's a good boy, though. Kind and gentle. He loves dogs. I'm so proud of him."

She bit her lower lip. For a second, I thought she might burst into tears. But Elsa was tough. All those trips over the years . . . all those competitions.

They made her what she was today, street-smart and savvy—and worldly—in ways most people, even if given a lifetime and then some, never could attain.

The drive to her parents' estate took less than an hour. Even before we pulled into the circle in front of the mansion, I could see the servants assembling to greet us. Then, as they unloaded the trunk, Liam took Thad into the house for hot cocoa. I helped Elsa out of the car.

"Won't you come in and have a cup of coffee?" she asked.

"That's very kind of you, but I think I should drive back to the city and get some sleep before jet lag catches up with me. That non-stop flight from Singapore was a killer!"

She looked at me through sad eyes and, with a catch in her voice, asked, "you know, don't you?"

I nodded, but said nothing.

"How long have you known?"

"Well, I wasn't sure at first. But then, when you and Liam brought him to the championship matches in Madrid last year and we all had dinner together, there was that moment—you know, that *fleeting* moment you experience just before your brain takes over and tries to convince you otherwise—when I thought, 'hmmm . . . I think Thad looks like me.' I don't know whether it was something I saw in his eyes or something I remembered from my old high school graduation picture. But in that instant, I saw something in him—"

She put a finger to my lips, and I stopped talking. Tears rolled down her face.

"Thad *is* your son, Jeff. Oh, how many times I wanted to tell you, believe me. But I *didn't* want you to think you had an obligation to me or to him. It was *my* decision to have a child. I was the one who deliberately went off the pill. Of all the men I knew and had been with, you were the *only* one I loved and respected. That's why I did what I did. For better or worse, I wanted you to be the father of my child. And regardless of how it would turn out, I had no intention—ever!—of asking you to shoulder any of the burden, financially or otherwise."

I was stunned. Yet, what she was saying, in a way, was something, deep down, I already had known. This had been her secret for more than 14 years, during which time we continued to share the intimate relationship I treasured so deeply. And, as she said, not once, despite the challenges she and her parents faced in raising Thad, did she ever ask me for anything, much less indicate I was the boy's father.

I handed her my handkerchief to dry her tears, meanwhile reaching out to embrace her.

"Jeff, I'm so sorry. I didn't mean to do this to you. I never intended to hurt you. It was so unfair of me. I hope you can find it in your heart to forgive me. But I'll understand if you want to walk away and never see me again--I really will. I know you never were given a choice. And as God is my witness, I wanted nothing from you. What more can I say than I'm sorry?"

We stood there, embracing, but saying nothing.

The secret was out, a secret she had kept from the man she loved, and, truth be told, from the man who loved her.

Finally, she stepped back, dabbed her eyes one last time, and handed me my handkerchief.

"Well," she said, "aren't you going to say something?"

"Sure. Is that offer of a cup of coffee still good?"

"Wet" (Photo: K. C. Brooks)
Indies Unlimited, January 19, 2019

"Are you sure it's out here?" I yelled to my guide.

25. Wet

"**A**re you sure it's out here?" I yelled to my guide, Major Gilbert Lambertson (ret.), a former fighter pilot with the Royal Australian Air Force.

"Sure 'n' my name is Gil," the elderly man replied, plowing on through the rock pools that remained at low tide off-shore of Darwin.

"Come on, mate," he yelled. "You're lookin' a mite stuffed at the moment!"

He laughed at my inability to keep up, all the while moving ahead at a pace that put me, some 30 years younger, to shame. Working a desk job with coffee and a Danish for breakfast obviously was not the best training for this excursion. Regardless, this early morning trek was a "must do" effort on my part.

Lambertson took a glance at his cell phone's GPS, made a small correction in the direction of our heading, and together, we trudged off down the coast until there it was, just around the bend: the exposed remnants of a B-25 Mitchell Bomber that again had been exposed in Darwin Harbour during a recent, violent storm.

I stood transfixed by what I saw. Before me were the remains of what surely was one of many of these twin-engine bombers to be found around here, the standard equipment for the Allied air forces in World War II.

"This one," said Lambertson, "carried two Australian and three Dutch airmen. Sadly, they never made it out alive.

"C'mon, let's go back; I'll take you to where they're buried."

See Endnote 8.

"Watson Lake" (Photo: K. S. Brooks)
Indies Unlimited, January 26, 2019

Prior to Lora's Disappearance, she reportedly lived
with one of her brothers and his family near Watson Lake, Yukon.

26. Watson Lake

"**So,** what is it you want to know about Loretta Frank?" asked retired RCMP captain Patrick McLean as he handed me a mug of steaming coffee.

I had trekked to his cabin near Lower Post, B.C., late in 2018, shortly after the first freeze, to obtain information for a newspaper story I was writing on aboriginal woman who disappeared or were murdered. Prior to Lora's disappearance—that's what her friends and family called her—she reportedly had lived with one of her brothers and his family near Watson Lake, Yukon.

"That's a tough one," replied the captain, taking a seat across from me. "I was assigned the case in 1995. The family insists they reported her missing within days of her disappearance in 1990, but for whatever reason, nothing had been done for five years."

"That doesn't sound good," I said.

"No, it doesn't. But truth be told, that's just the way things were back then. And besides, given her medical history—"

"Her medical history?"

"Well, the poor woman, only 19 at the time, had been diagnosed with schizophrenia. Social services tried to help but never was able to treat her. And then, she started moving around, first to Whitehorse, and, after moving home briefly, returning to Whitehorse, where she apparently met some guy from Haines, Alaska. That's the last anyone heard from her.

"When I retired, hers was just one of more than 200 indigenous women missing persons cases on the books. It was overwhelming."

See Footnote 9.

"The Path Beside Shady Brook" (Photo: Susan Cohen)

I took a walk today beside the brook near our home.

27. The Path Beside Shady Brook

I took a walk today beside the brook near our home.

The thermometer had pushed into the 60s. Can you believe it, for the first week in February?! And to think: only days ago we awoke to a temperature of 3, with a wind chill of -15. Not that we could complain. My sister in Chicago said the temperature was -15 with a wind chill of -50. That's what she gets for living in the Windy City, I said, though I joked it was her politicians who were "windy," not the weather.

Here, as they say, spring was in the air. Literally. It struck me as soon as I stepped from the door, that unique scent I often had experienced as a boy growing up in Wisconsin during the 1940s.

I don't know how to describe it as anything but what I smelled on my way to school in early March, when winter's iron-fisted grip on our lives finally was broken and the snow started to melt, revealing Mother Earth in all her glory. Here and there the shoots of the first daffodils or crocuses had begun to emerge and with them, signs of life renewed.

Scientists have given us all manner of explanations for the "smell of spring": the evaporation of thawed moisture, the revival of trees, bacteria on the surface (the wet earth smell of geosmin). It matters not. To me, it's the scent of memories treasured.

I took a walk today beside the brook near our home.

See Footnote 10.

"Disappeared" (Photo: Tverdokhlib, Big Stock Photo)

"And you never saw after that Tuesday?" I asked.

28. Disappeared

"**A**nd you never saw after that Tuesday?" I asked, setting my beer on the bar and taking out a fresh pack of Marlboros.

"Nope, and that's what's so disturbing. It's like she never existed. One day she was there—I saw her for lunch that day, remember?!—and Wednesday, when I took a cab to her place to pick her up—we were supposed to take a mid-morning train into New York City to see a matinee performance on Broadway—she was gone."

I tapped the pack of cigarettes on the back of my wrist, removed the cellophane and foil on one end, knocked out a few cigarettes, and, selecting one, lit it. Taking a drag, I slowly released the smoke into the blue-gray air above the bar.

Josh sat for a minute, staring into the huge mirror in front of us and rubbing his chin. "It makes no sense, Brian. We talked Tuesday night before I went to sleep. She was excited about seeing the show, that's for sure. She did say she had to run into the office early Wednesday morning to drop off a final report her group had finally completed, but she promised she'd be back to her apartment in plenty of time to meet me when I showed up. In fact, she said she'd be downstairs, waiting.

"We even had plans to have dinner in the city after the performance before catching a late train for home at Penn Station. Frankly, it would've been the perfect day!

"But when I got to her apartment around 9 that morning, she wasn't there. And she didn't answer the doorman's ring. Even stranger, he said he never even saw her leave the building that morning.

"I tried calling her at work, but the receptionist said she'd never come in. In fact, according to the receptionist, they, too, had become concerned. She was always so good about letting them know her plans, and they were depending on her to deliver that final report by the opening of business that morning.

"Well, did they try calling her?"

"Oh, yes, but their calls went unanswered."

"Okay, so when did all this happen?"

"More than a week ago."

"*A week ago?!* Are you freakin' kidding me?! And you haven't heard a word from her since that Tuesday night?"

"Nope. Neither has her office. And she'd been with the company for three years, which really surprised them. But then, when I talked to the woman in Human Resources, she said some employees and especially new hires were 'ghosting' them right and left these days. I guess the labor market is so tight people literally will jump ship at the drop of a hat."

"But Samira—that was her name, right?"

"Yeah, but I called her Sammy"

"Okay, but Sammy didn't seem like the flighty type, did she? At least that's the impression you gave me. I got the feeling she was one of these young, independent professionals out to make to make a name for herself in the advertising world.

"That's right. Her parents were immigrants from the Middle East—Saudis, I think. Dissidents, she said, but not particularly outspoken against the regime. She once mentioned both were doctors, and though they had a bit of rough time gaining a toehold in the US, they finally established themselves, put Sammy and her sister through college, and—"

"Sounds fairly normal to me."

"Yeah, I think so. And the strange thing is, Sammy had recently received a promotion to the head of her department. Quite the move, I must say, and the pay to go with it."

Josh finished his beer and signaled the bartender for a refill.

"So, "I asked, passing on a refill, "did you file a missing person report with the local police at the time?"

"Oh, yeah, within two days. A helluva lot of good that did. I even gave them a picture of Sammy I'd taken a month earlier." He pulled his wallet from the back pocket of his trousers and showed me a print of the picture he'd given to the police. "I gave her those hoop earrings for her 25th birthday.

"The detective I spoke with said they'd keep everything in their active files. But he added that without additional information or evidence of foul play, it would be difficult for them to devote resources to a search. As he said, she's an adult, free to come and go as she pleases, so chances are good she may simply have decided to take off and do something different."

"Take off and do something different? Give me a break! People don't just 'take off and do something different' without a good reason, especially if they have a good job, just received a promotion, have their own furnished apartment, are in a great relationship, have major social plans for that day, and the like."

"I know, I know, Brian. You don't have to tell me. It makes no sense. And get this. I went back to her apartment building yesterday—you know, just to nose around, talk to some people who lived there, assuming I could catch them at the front door, and so forth. I got into a conversation with the doorman. He told me the building's super went into her apartment to check up on her a few days after I was to have picked her up. And then he said the strangest thing: when the super entered her apartment, he found the place as clean as a whistle."

"Well, there musta been signs she'd lived there. She'd only been gone a few days."

"No. Not a thing! Her personal stuff'd been completely cleaned out. There wasn't a shred of evidence she'd *ever* lived there. Not only that, the super told him it was like someone had gone through the entire apartment with an industrial cleaning crew. All of the furniture had been thoroughly cleaned and the floors vacuumed, and the bathroom and kitchen were spotless. He said the management office could've put the place up for rent *that* day, and he wouldn't have to do another thing to get it ready.

"I'm telling you, Brian, he made it sound like Sammy was 'disappeared.' "

I ashed my cigarette in the porcelain tray on the counter, took one last drag on the butt, and stubbed it out.

"And your date that Wednesday would have been on October?—"

Josh picked up his cell phone, keyed up a calendar, took it to late 2018, and said, "October 3rd."

"Jesus, that's the day after Jamal Khashoggi—you know *The Washington Post's* journalist—was killed in the Saudi Embassy in Istanbul."

"Come on, Brian, you don't think the two things are connected, do ya?" Josh asked, his face turning ashen.

"Well, you said her parents were dissidents. How much do you *really* know about their *and her* activities?"

"Not a helluva lot, that's for sure," Josh replied, laying his head on his arms, which a moment earlier he had folded on the bar.

For a minute neither of us said anything.

Then, Josh raised his head, turned, and said. "Do ya think she's okay, Brian. I mean, she's only 25. I know she's an adult, but still—"

"I'm sure there's a logical answer, Josh. There *must* be one, for sure!

"Meanwhile, my advice to you is, contact the FBI."

"The Girl in the Rowboat" (Photo: Pinterest)

"I have something to show you," she said, reaching into her purse
and withdrawing a weathered photograph of a sailor
and his girlfriend in a rowboat.

29. The Girl in the Rowboat

"Dad? Dad, are you awake?"

The woman gently shook the elderly man's shoulder as she prepared to spend time with him early one spring morning. Sunlight filtered through the curtains covering the French doors bordering the nursing center's central visiting area, brightening the room and giving it a sense of life renewed.

"Huh? What?" mumbled the disoriented man, awakening from his sleep. Then, seeing his daughter, he relaxed, smiled, closed his eyes for a moment, and, though he appeared to drift back to sleep, murmured, "thank you for coming. I missed you."

"I missed you, too, Dad," she said softly, setting her coat aside. Pulling up a chair, she sat beside him, brushed some loose hairs back from his forehead, and, picking up a cup of water from the table next to him, offered him a drink. He took several sips through the straw, wiped his mouth with the back of his hand, and settled back in his wheelchair.

"I have something to show you," she said, reaching into her purse and withdrawing a weathered photograph of a sailor and his girlfriend in a rowboat. "I found this among Mom's things when I was cleaning out her closet this morning. It was in a small cigar box full of photographs and letters she kept under some sweaters in the bottom drawer of her clothes cabinet. Have you seen it before? I'm sure that's her in the boat, but I haven't the faintest idea who that's with her. There's a handwritten note on the back, and even though the ink's faded, I think it says it was taken in Central Park sometime in 1940."

The old man laughed. "That's Georgie Porgie Pudding and Pie!"

"Come on, Dad, get serious," his daughter demanded anxiously, worried her father might be "losing it."

"No, seriously. That's what I used to call him when they were dating. Your mother hated it when I said that!

107

"Remember, your Mom and I attended college in New York City at that time. On weekends she used to dress to the nine, head for Broadway, and pick up anything in a uniform for some fun on the town.

"His name was George Anderson. She had a crush on him, and I have to say, I think he loved her as well. He didn't get to the Port of New York often, but when he did, she'd disappear for days.

"And then, in 1943, word came he was missing in action—his destroyer was escorting a convoy across the North Atlantic when it was torpedoed south of Iceland with the loss of all hands."

He motioned toward the water with his fingers, and she held the cup for him while he took a few sips through the straw.

"That must've been difficult for her," his daughter said, dabbing his mouth with a tissue.

"She was inconsolable. For a while, she returned to running around the city and chasing anything in a uniform that batted an eye at her, just to help her forget George. She even dropped out of school for a semester. But her parents convinced her to return, and slowly, she recovered her 'balance'. In time, we began a relationship that blossomed into love.

"But in all the years we were married—and those were 70 of the happiest years I have known—I don't think she *ever* got over losing him. I'll tell you this, a man could not have asked for a more loving woman to share his life, but sure as I'm sitting here, I'm positive she thought of him *every day of hers.*"

"But you had a great life together, didn't you, Dad? I mean, you don't have any regrets, do you?"

"No, honey, I have no regrets. We got married the day after she graduated from college, and we made a good life for ourselves on Wall Street. The city had so much to offer, and we took advantage of it at every turn. But then, it was time to turn down the flame, and central Pennsylvania seemed like a nice place to retire.

"I have to tell you, though, at first it seemed like a foreign country to us. Old buildings, some colleges, museums, restaurants . . . mixed bag . . . one room school houses in the countryside, hunters on the land in the fall . . . a good pastor in the country church, some professionals on their land estates, farmers, businessmen in their closed communities, mostly Germans and Pennsylvania Dutch to be found everywhere, and of course, everyone with stories of happiness and tears. But we all got along, trying to help each other and laugh as much as possible.

"I have no nostalgia for our old townhouse in the city, with the unfriendly, hostile neighbors, peeling wallpaper, and total dependence on trades people. Couldn't even own a car, not that you needed one. I do miss the walks around the streets, though . . . and along the shore. Ah, yes . . . the shore. But it's being destroyed, slowly, or not so slowly, when a big storm comes along. And, of course, after my brain tumor and surgery, my balance isn't what it used to be, so even if I were able to use a walker, I wouldn't be able to get around too good.

"But still, you do what you can do, right?"

He turned and looked at her with a wistful look in his eyes. Whether it was because of things he had left unsaid over a lifetime or undone when her mother was alive was something she couldn't determine. But it seemed to her the picture of his wife with the woman's true first love had rekindled memories of that time just before the world went mad when the three of them—his wife, George Anderson, and he—were about to embark on what seemed, at the time, a period of unlimited opportunities.

"No, *I* have no regrets, honey," he said, laughing. "But on the day she died, your mother told me there were two things *she* deeply regretted never having done."

"What were they, Dad?"

"Tangoed in a red satin ruffled dress and waltzed in black velvet."

"Alley" (Photo: K. S. Brooks)
Indies Unlimited, February 16, 2019

"Are you sure that is where she went after leaving your taxi?"

30. Alley

"**A**re your sure that is where she went after leaving your taxi?"

"*Si, señor.* Very sure. I was driving up Calle de la Fortaleza when she suddenly yelled at me to stop. '*¡Detén el coche!*' she yelled. I don't know what made her change her mind, *señor*, because when I picked her up at the church a few minutes earlier, she told me to drive to her cruise ship *muy rápidamente.* She kept mumbling about the ship leaving without her.

"Anyway, I slammed on the brakes and swerved to the curb. She threw five dollars at me, opened the door, and jumped out. It is not good for a *gringo* lady to walk by herself on the streets when it is getting dark, so I followed her—at a distance, of course—and saw her run up Calle de la Cruz to this alley. Then, she ran to the green building at the back."

"Are you positive she went to the green building?"

"*Si, señor.* I saw her pound on the door several times. Finally, someone opened it. It was a man, I'm sure of that. He looked around like he wanted to make sure she wasn't being followed. Then, he pulled her inside and slammed the door.

"Why are you asking all these questions, *señor?*"

"Because we found her body floating in Bahia de San Juan this morning, off Puerta de Tierra, next to the man listed as the owner of that green building."

"Farewell to a Friend" (Photo: Claudia Lee Malone)
William Alden Lee, 1933 - 2019

I first met Retired U.S. Navy Commander Willian Alden (Bill) Lee,
then of Frederick, Maryland, late of Doylestown, Pennsylvania,
when he called me in 1994.

31. Farewell to a Friend

"I first met retired U.S. Navy Commander Willian Alden (Bill) Lee, then of Frederick, Maryland, late of Doylestown, Pennsylvania, when he called me in 1994—literally out of the blue, as they say—to discuss a letter to the editor I wrote that had been published in *The Washington Post*. At the time, I lived in Waynewood, near Mt. Vernon, Virginia.

Bill agreed with what I had stated in the letter. Our conversation led to lunch at Washington, DC's, Union Station during that year's Christmas season. What followed was a friendship that extended over 25 years and included moves on both our parts to southeastern Pennsylvania. It was a period punctuated by constant exchanges of e-mails, mail postings from Bill (packed with newspaper articles he thought I'd find of interest), and later, twice-yearly meetings at his residence, given Bill's inability to drive because he suffered from ataxia.

Our e-mail conversations and those over lunch touched on classical music, politics, American history, and literature. Bill was a stickler for proper grammar, so I wasn't surprised when he offered to become my editor. Now, we embarked on yet another "journey" in which he wielded his rapierlike pen against the typos and other grammatical insults that assaulted him as he poured through countless drafts of my novels, short stories, pieces of flash fiction, and illustrated children's books. *Bill was thrilled!* Not that he lacked for editing challenges. Based on my reads of the e-mails he sent to the editors of *The New York Times*, *The Washington Post*, and *The Wall Street Journal*, they had been feeling the sting of his pen's nib for years!

Alas, time caught up with Bill on March 28, 2019, stilling his voice—and his pen—forever. I'll miss talking to him, opening his thick repurposed envelopes bursting at the seams with newspaper articles, and, most of all, acting upon his detailed edits to my scribblings . . . directions to fix the spelling of this or that word or, for example, to check the second sentence of the penultimate paragraph for an incorrect pronoun reference. Edits like these were part and parcel of his work, and he was dogged in the pursuit of perfection. When it came to editing, his nickname, "The Scrubber," was well-deserved!

I cited Bill's contributions to my writings in my books' **Acknowledgements** sections, of course, giving generous thanks to "my earnest grammarian and long-suffering editor." In this volume, for which Bill only had been able to edit half of the stories before he passed, the **Acknowledgements** section, unfortunately, must read in part: "to my erstwhile editor."

I'll miss you, Bill, for ever many reasons, but mostly because we were like brothers who shared a common world of thoughts, ideas, and visions for what the world could be.

"Stink Eye" (Photo: K. S. Brooks)
Indies Unlimited, February 23, 2019

"Whatcha lookin' at?!" asked Sheri, the deer closest
to the photographer.

32. Stink Eye

hatcha lookin' at?!" asked Sheri, the deer closest to the photographer.

"I didn't mean to—"

"No, of course not. You were just standing there, staring at us for no good reason. Is there a problem?"

"Well, you *were* standing by the side of the road. And given I didn't know whether you were going stay there or leap in front of my car, causing an accident—"

"Whoa, whoa, whoa, sister. Hang on a gosh darn minute. I wanna make sure we get this straight. You—in your fancy, schmancy, little red roadster—were barreling down this nice, quiet dirt road like a bat out of Hell while we're standing here, minding our own business, nibbling a little dew-covered grass, and it's *our* fault *you* had to stand your car on its nose?"

Sheri turned to Marybelle on her right, stuck her nose in the air, and let out a derisive laugh.

"You tell her," Marybelle responded.

"Well," said the driver, "we live here too, just down the road in one of the new homes built last year."

The three deer laughed.

"You call those McMansions homes?" snorted Cindy on Sheri's left.

"Cindy!" snapped Marybelle. "If you can't say something nice, don't say anything at all!"

Cindy nodded, chagrined. "You're right." She turned to the driver and, with head bowed, said: "They all have beautiful gardens. We especially love eating the blue plantain lilies."

117

"Waiting" (Photo, K. S. Brooks; Model, Ryan O'Crotty)
Indies Unlimited, March 2, 2019

"Oh, that's Peter . . . he was my fiancée."

33. Waiting

"**W**ho's this?" her neighbor asked, turning the page in the album and wiping her fingers across the clear plastic sheet that covered the photograph of a man atop a mountain who appeared to be waiting for someone to catch up with him. The neatly typed note pasted beneath the photo read: Organ Mountains, February, 2017.

Her host looked wistfully at the photograph and, for a moment, said nothing.

"Oh, that's Peter . . . he was my fiancée."

On hearing that, the large German Shepherd at her feet, his eyes wide open, raised his head.

"Peter was temporarily stationed at Ft. Bliss prior to shipping out for Afghanistan on his third deployment."

The dog put his head down between his paws and seemingly went to sleep. Every now and then, though, something his mistress said caused him to open his eyes and whimper softly.

"Jethro, here, worked with Peter as an explosive detector dog," the woman said at one point. "They were working a village search and security operation in the Dand area of Kandahar Province of southern Afghanistan when Jethro 'alerted' to an IED. Peter attempted to disarm it so the rest of the task force could pass, but the device exploded, killing him and severely injuring Jethro. Peter's comrades in arms made sure Jethro was airlifted to a field hospital for surgery, and following his recovery, they sent him home to me.

"He—and this photograph—are all I have now to remind me of Peter."

"Stefan" (Photo: Roger Rössing; Wikimedia Commons,
public domain)

Another garage, in an alley several blocks away, was home to four
ponies. Shetland mares all, they were owned by the father of my friend,
Stefan.

34. Stefan

"I remember well the alleys and garages around our home on North Seventeenth Street in Milwaukee in the years immediately following WWII; they never ceased to pique my interest.

Up the alley behind our duplex near the garage where Dad parked the family's maroon Custom Clipper Packard sedan—Dad always drove Packards—was the garage where the local ragman stabled his horse and stored his wagon. Beyond that, another neighbor garaged the bright red midget race car that he took to weekend track events in southern Wisconsin and northern Illinois. Mother said the men were "unsavory," whatever that meant, but it never kept me from talking to them. Besides, I loved feeding apples to the ragman's horse late in the afternoon, after practicing the piano, while the old man unloaded his cart after returning from a day loading up whatever rags, old clothes, and other items of value he had acquired on the city's west side.

Another garage, in an alley several blocks away, was home to four ponies. Shetland mares all, they were owned by the father of my friend, Stefan. The ponies were his father's; he—with Stefan's help—gave children rides on Sundays at local parks on the north and west sides of the city. I was fascinated! I mean, can you imagine walking into a car garage in the middle of a city and finding four ponies? For a boy of 8, it was a dream come true!

So, I sometimes sneaked over to visit Stefan and the ponies on my way home from school before running home to practice the piano. Occasionally, when no one else was around, Stefan would let him sit on one of the gentler ones, easily distinguished from the others by her shiny black coat and a white star under her forelock. I named him Star. On hindsight, that wasn't the most imaginable of names, but hey, give me credit for my adventuresome spirit and ability to make the most of my free-range childhood.

"Come on, Stefan, let's play some stickball[8] in the alley before I have to go home," I'd often would call when I got within earshot of the little stable.

"Can't, Teddy," was Stefan's forlorn reply more often than not. "Must muck stable."

Stefan did not speak English well. His family, like several others in his neighborhood, immigrated to the United States from Eastern Europe with the help of the Roman Catholic Church following World War II. The fact is, he and his little sister, Kasienka, were the only two in their family who spoke much English, and only then because of having attended public school.

Stefan's father, a janitor, worked two jobs during the week while his mother cleaned houses for women on Milwaukee's East Side. Stefan and Kasienka attended Brown Street Grade School, so, at least during the day, their parents did not have to worry about them. But after school, it was Stefan's job to muck out the stable as soon as he got home. This left precious little time for him to do anything else before he, his sister, and their mother sat down to dinner, which almost always consisted of bigos[9] and home-baked bread with szmalec.[10] (I tried the bread once and found it heavy, with a strange acid taste.)

At least once monthly and always on a Friday evening, the ladies from St. Michael's Catholic Church dropped by with a chicken and pork dish that Stefan's mother saved for Sunday's dinner, the only time the family ate together. Neighbors knew when the church delegation had dropped by with dinner because on those occasions, Stefan's mother changed the orientation of the large preprinted ice card[11] posted in the family's front-room window as a

---

[8] A pick-up game played in a street or alley; it was similar to baseball but played with a broom handle and rubber ball.

[9] Polish stew made of meat and cabbage

[10] Polish lard; also called the "poor man's butter"

[11] The ice card was employed by people who literally used ice boxes to keep meats and other perishables cold; the card's purpose was to tell the ice delivery man how many pounds of ice they needed on any given day. (http://wcgs.ala.nu/icecard.htm)

sign to the ice deliveryman that she needed an extra twenty-five pounds when he brought his horse-drawn wagon up their street the following morning.

Though Stefan and I were about the same age, he was slightly shorter and lighter in weight than I. His dirty blond hair and blue eyes stood in sharp contrast to my reddish-brown hair and hazel eyes. Stefan's clothes were ill-fitting hand-me-downs—everything he wore, in fact, had been given to his family by Catholic Social Services of the Archdiocese of Milwaukee. His mother repaired his socks with a darning needle and yarn, and she did the wash several times each week before retiring in the evening so that her children were never without clean clothes for school. Stefan's brown shoes, always untied, had not seen polish since the day they were given to him by the Church.

I, on the other hand, never lacked for new clothes or shoes, when these were required.

From the outside, then, it would be difficult to find two more unlikely friends. Our differences, however significant they might appear to some, were of no import. For us, the only thing that mattered was our friendship.

I felt sorry for Stefan. Sometimes, I would bring Stefan the Babe Ruth candy bar or Superman comic my grandfather, Grandpa Joe, had purchased for me after my Monday night piano lesson. Stefan always was appreciative. But I knew there was little I could do to help him. Though young, he already had sensed life was not fair, that no matter how hard a person might try, it was possible to control everything—or even to have a significant impact on the lives of others.

To this day, the mere scent of a pony or a horse evokes memories of that stable and time in my life. And it leaves me wondering: what became of Stefan and Kasienka.

See Endnote 11.

"Stakeout" (Photo: endomotion, Big Stock Photo)

This was the third night we had been holed up in the apartment above the used furniture store on Atlantic Avenue in Brooklyn.

35. Stakeout

T his was the third night we had been holed up in the apartment above the used furniture store on Atlantic Avenue in Brooklyn. It was 8 p.m. on a chilly November evening. Minutes earlier we had relieved Detectives Eddy Lewis and Mary Fitzpatrick, who had been assigned to cover the previous 12-hour shift. The furniture store had been closed for hours and the street lamps were in full bloom. The NYPD was using this location to stake out what appeared to be an abandoned business establishment. An anonymous tip suggested members of an Iranian foundation linked to the assassination of a Wall Street banker in late October met here.

We were using twin, 35mm digital SLR cameras with ten-megapixel image sensors and manual exposure settings. Both were focused on the entrance to the storefront. The building's windows were covered with butcher paper, but, at the least, we were looking for opportunities to capture images of people entering and leaving the building as well as shots of vehicles of interest.

Despite the fact it was cold outside, we kept the apartment window 'cracked', just to make sure we didn't miss anything happening on the street if, for some reason, both of us happened to be looking away or were otherwise distracted for a moment.

"Tell me again what we know about these people, Lou?" asked Detective Sean O'Keeffe as he checked the cameras for the second time to ensure they were properly aimed and focused.

"It's probably an Iranian front organization," I responded. "The chief said the foundation was registered in the Jebel Ali Free Zone, which is located in the United Arab Emirates. It's only 21 miles southwest of Dubai City and built around Port Rashid, the world's largest man-made port."

"Nice way to hide one's pedigree."

"I'll say. The majority of business in the Free Zone is done by small traders whose names aren't well known. And it doesn't take more than a glance at any map of the area to show you that it's only a hop, skip, and a jump from Port

Rashid to Bandar-e Lengeh, the closest port in Iran. The chief said a person in a high-speed boat could get money and goods that had been shipped to the Jebel Ali Free Zone into Iran in no time. In fact, despite the US embargo on shipments to Iran, trade between the Free Zone and Iran isn't prohibited. There are plenty of companies in the Free Zone that will transship goods to Iran."

"So, this 'Iranian foundation', for all we know, is just a front to move money to Iran in violation of the sanctions we've imposed. Or worse. Hell, they could be funding terrorist organizations directly, for all we know!"

"Bingo! It's not clear how that banker got caught up in the mix, but one thing's for sure: he's dead. One slug through the heart at close range! And the killer's trail leads directly to the shop across the street."

I had no sooner finished speaking when we heard a car door slam. Turning our attention to the window, we observed a lone figure making his way quickly to the building across the street. Sean clicked the shutters of both cameras multiple times, capturing, in rapid succession, sequential images of what appeared to be a man, who, having stepped to the door, first turned to assure himself that no one had seen him, and then, using his key, opened the door and quickly made his way inside.

"What the fu—" I whispered, rubbing my chin.

Sean turned and gave me a quizzical look. "You look like you're seen a ghost? Do you recognize him?"

"Let me see one of those cameras."

He handed me one. I was startled by what I saw in the camera's display screen. Did I know the guy? Hell, I knew him well.

We first met in kindergarten and were inseparable through our senior year of high school. His name was Vince—Vince Ponticelli. Now, he appeared to be about five-ten, 190 pounds, and stout. In high school, however, he was trim and muscular, and sported a full head of pitch-black hear worn in a mullet. A liberal application of Dippity-do was *de rigor* in those days, as was his daily attire consisting of a cotton t-shirt, black jeans, and biker boots.

Even as a kid Vince knew *everything* that went on in Brooklyn, especially if it was the least bit on the shady side. This knowledge, and the people with whom he associated, affected him greatly. It wasn't long before his own life took a turn to the dark side. On the bottom shelf of the bookcase in his bedroom, for example, were four books he had ostensibly used in high school: books on civics, science, algebra, and Spanish. Ponticelli glued them together at the end of our sophomore year, then hollowed out the inside of the stack to form a hiding place for marijuana. His parents never suspected he had the drug, which he sold to friends and acquaintances. I have to admit, too, that in our junior and senior years, he and I used to enjoy a joint now and then, especially after we took our dates home on Saturday night.

"The guy never had a chance," I muttered. "Not that I was a saint. I got into a lot of trouble, most of it with Vince—I mean, you wouldn't believe the things we pulled until my old man, God rest his soul—he was a street cop you know—finally had enough. He grabbed me by the ear after my high school graduation, marched me down to the Army recruiter, and forced me to enlist. I ended up at Fort Rucker in the US Army Aviation Center. You know the rest."

"So, what happened to Vince? Obviously, you haven't been in touch with him."

"Well, I tried talking him into coming into the Army with me, but his parents, with four other mouths to feed, insisted he get a job close to home and start helping out with the family. Vince went down to the docks and found himself a job as a longshoreman. It came with a terrible price, though, because he got involved with the mob.

"On top of that, he got his girlfriend Elena pregnant, which complicated their lives beyond anything you can imagine. Not only did they have to get married, but each of their parents threw them out.

I handed Sean the camera, which he remounted on its tripod and again aimed at the storefront across the street.

"Steph tried to stay in touch with Elena," I continued. "They also were high school classmates. But the tougher things got for her and Vince, the more difficult it was for Steph to learn what was happening.

"Anyway, the last time I heard about Vince was in a letter Steph wrote to me when I was flying Black Hawk combat missions out of Kuwait, something to the effect Elena and Vince's son had died of cancer."

"God, that musta been rough!"

127

"Ya think? The kid's name was Joey. Elena told Steph he'd been battling leukemia for several years. They thought it was in remission, but then, he died a week short of his tenth birthday. Elena told Steph that watching Joey suffer destroyed Vince. He couldn't take it anymore, she said, and he left them six months before the kid passed."

"Wait! You're telling me the kid's dying, and the guy leaves his wife to deal with it? What the Hell?"

"I know. I couldn't believe it either."

Sean shook his head. "Damn, what goes through some people's minds? How do you leave your wife to deal with something like that?!"

"That's a good question, my friend, a very good question. Let's ask right after we bust him and read 'im his rights."

See **Endnote 12.**

"Molly" (Photo: michelangeloop, Big Stock Photo)

"I seem to remember a certain, special young woman. What was
her name?"
"Ah, you must be talking about Molly . . . Molly Patterson."

36. Molly

"**S**teve? Steve Jennings?"

"Dan Rollins! Well, I'll be go to hell! Is that really you? My god, what's it been, 50 years?"

The two men shook hands, then embraced in a bear hug before sitting at the bar in Madison's Edgewater Hotel, not far from the state capitol.

"What's your poison?" asked Rollins, signaling to the bartender, who already was making his way toward them."

"Oh, the usual . . . Jack Daniel's on the rocks. Smooth as it comes."

"Make that two," said Rollins to the bartender, who had overheard the conversation and proceeded to set two napkins and a dish of peanuts in front of the men.

"You got it, Mr. Rollins," replied the bartender, who obviously knew his customer.

"So, Steve" continued Dan," what brings you back to the scene of our youthful indiscretions?"

"Well, it *has* been 50 years since we graduated. So, when the class of '66 reached out and issued invitations for the 50th reunion, I thought, what the hell, it might be great to see some of the old haunts again. You know, Bascom Hill, the Brathaus, Rennebohm's drug *store* . . . places like that. But I never expected to see you here."

"Oh, heck, I never left," replied Dan. "Just stayed put and continued working for the real estate firm that employed me part-time when I was in college. I ended up buying the company in 1983, Made quite a good living for Judy and me, too, and—"

"Hey, that's right. I remember you were dating Judy all through our junior and senior years. Man, you were a lucky guy. She always reminded me of Natalie Wood. How *is* she?"

"Judy passed away three years ago, Steve. Ovarian cancer. It had already progressed to stage IV when they detected it. By then, it was too late; there was nothing they could do. She died a month later."

"I'm so sorry, Dan," said Steve, shaking his head. "That must've been difficult."

They sat in silence for several seconds, broken only by the bartender arriving with their drinks.

"Here you go, gents. How we doin' on the peanuts?"

"We're good, Joe" replied Dan, giving him a weak smile.

The men picked up their drinks and before Dan could speak, Steve toasted: "To Judy."

"To Judy," Dan replied.

The men sipped their whiskeys.

"Anyway," continued Dan, "you wouldn't recognize our little city today, that's for sure."

"I'll say. I took a quick tour around the campus and Fraternity Row on my way from the airport, Frankly, I had a tough time making my way around the area. You can't drive on State Street anymore. What's up with that?"

"Isn't that a hoot?" Dan replied. "City vehicles, pedestrians, and bikes only."

"I also tried to find the house we used to live in on North Francis. Remember? We had that little apartment on the third floor. It didn't even have a shower; that was to be found on the second floor and was used by everybody in the building."

"You bet. That was the house next to the church of Holy Rollers. Remember how they used to 'rock out' during Sunday night services?"

"Do I! Well, I can tell you this, the old house is gone. So much for *those* good memories."

"So, what about you?" asked Dan, sipping his whiskey. "Last I heard, you'd been commissioned as a second lieutenant in the Army and were off to the war. At that point, you evaporated into thin air."

"Yeah, sorry about that. Things got a little hectic once I went on active duty. The war in Nam was heating up, as you recall, and within two days of being commissioned, the Army shipped my ass to Ft. Gordon for two months of post-ROTC Signal Officer training. From there I got assigned to support to the comm center at Tan Son Nhut Air Base. Man, did we take a shellacking in December of that year. You're lucky you were 4F, my friend. That was no party over there."

"Sorry, buddy. Would have been right there with you if it hadn't been for my ticker," Dan replied sheepishly.

Steve, sipping his drink, waved his hand as if to say *forget it*. Then he grabbed a handful of peanuts, popped them into his mouth, and continued. "Anyway, I put in three tours in Nam over ten years. By the end of February, 1975, I'd made lieutenant colonel and was assigned as the chief signal officer in the US Embassy in Saigon."

"The end of February?" Dan couldn't believe his ears. "Are you freakin' kidding me? Then you musta been there when the city fell that April?"

"Of course I was there. Shit! I was *in* the goddamn embassy as the Viet Cong were moving on the compound. That could be me you see in some photos, helping people climb into those Huey's that were touching down on the roof long enough for us to load them up and get 'em on their way out to sea."

"Jesus!"

"Well, there wasn't much more I could do. I mean, I'd already torched all of the classified documents and destroyed the comm center's communications and crypto equipment. Might as well help out on the roof before getting out of Dodge. The embassy was supposed to have been the secondary evacuation point for embassy personnel, but in the end, it was overwhelmed with desperate South Vietnamese. I barely made it out with the shirt on my back. Hundreds were left behind.

"I finally ended up on the *USS Midway*. There were so many Hueys inbound, flown by both US and RVN pilots, that as soon as one landed, the ship's crew pushed it overboard to make way for the next. What a disaster. It finally got so bad we were radioing pilots to drop off passengers and then, take off and ditch at sea. We had boats waiting to rescue the pilots, of course. I had nightmares for years after that."

Steve shook his head and took another sip from his glass.

"Wow," remarked Dan, "that's quite a story. Thank you for your service, old friend! Who would have thought you had it in you, given all the stuff you pulled in your college days."

"What do you mean 'all the stuff I pulled in my college days'?" Steve responded, laughing.

"Just saying," said Dan, with a wry grin on his face. "I seem to remember a certain, special young woman— What was her name?"

"Ah, you must be talking about Molly . . . Molly Patterson."

"Yes, that's the lass. I remember how, all too often, I would come back to our apartment after lunch, only to find your shoes outside the door, letting me know you and Molly were, shall we say, enjoying an afternoon delight and I should cool my heels elsewhere."

Steve laughed. "Actually, I put the shoes out there hoping the building's valet would shine them. But I have to tell you, I'd take an afternoon with Molly over a three-hour electronics lab any day of the week."

"Well, by my reckoning, you did. Frequently. Fact is, I don't know how you *ever* made the grades you did while you two were dating. So, did you ever make an honest woman of her?"

"Sadly, no. And you know, Dan, even after all those years together, I still can't figure out what happened. We went steady from the time we were sophomores, we both loved children, and I figured we'd get married at some point. We talked about it . . . she knew that the life of an Army officer's wife might not be the easiest, with long separations, frequent moves, and all that. But we were in love, and we figured we could make it work.

"Then, after graduation, she went back to New York, and I went on active duty. We corresponded for a while, but it wasn't long before she stopped writing. I don't know if she met someone, whether her parents put the kibosh on our relationship—I always got the feeling they weren't keen on me, my being from the Midwest and all—if the Army was a put-off, or what. But it got to the point where she simply stopped writing, and I figured it was time to move on."

Dan signaled the bartender for another round. Upon its arrival he proposed a toast: "To Molly."

"To Molly," responded Steve. "I hope she's happy somewhere."

"Bridge" (Photo: K. S. Brooks)

She could hear the sound of a fog horn in the background.

37. Bridge

"**It's** no good, Ashley."

She heard the desperation in his voice. She'd heard it before—many times—and it never ended well, not for him nor for her.

This time she could hear the sound of a fog horn in the background. Ships' horns, too.

"Where are you, Tony?"

"What does it matter?" His words were slurred. He had been drinking.

He burst into tears. "God knows I've tried, Ashley . . . I've tried so hard. Not only for you, but for me, too. I think of what we had and what could have been, and—"

His voice dissolved into sobs, sobs so deep and violent his entire body shook.

The line went silent.

"Tony? Tony!" she yelled in desperation. "Don't do it!"

"What difference would it make? It's always the same old story. Everything's fine for a little while after rehab, and then, something goes wrong, and it's only the drugs that seem to make it better. But they don't, and before you know it, we're right back to where we started . . . more rehab, more drugs, and then, back into rehab again. It just never ends."

Their lives hadn't always been like this, full of irrational outbursts, tirades, and threats.   Earlier, to friends, acquaintances, and associates alike, their marriage appeared to be perfect. Everyone had called them blessed. They were a handsome couple with two beautiful children who often vacationed in southern France aboard a friend's yacht. Both had earned master's degrees—with honors—from one the nation's most prestigious business school and by 2000, each had made partner in their firm, two the largest financial institutions on Wall Street. Known for their generous contributions to the city's many charities, it wasn't unusual to find the couple among weekend crowds at the Met or Carnegie Hall. They seemingly had it all!

Ashley Kensington and Anthony Thurston "Tony" Webster II, who grew up in Stamford, Connecticut, had dated since their junior year in high school. Some said it was preordained they would marry after college—both had attended Harvard—and. indeed, they did. Their wedding, attended by a veritable Who's Who of financial and banking professionals, sported a guest list that numbered in the hundreds It was the talk of The Hamptons for months, both before *and* after the ceremony.

Following a two-week honeymoon in the Seychelle Islands, the couple settled into their Fifth Avenue penthouse apartment on Manhattan's Upper East Side and, except for Ashley's relatively brief maternity leaves following the births of their two children, they both worked full time in the city's Financial District. That a full-time nanny watched over the children while a maid tended to the apartment obviously made their lives easier. That said, however, the couple were loving parents who often could be found in Central Park on the weekends, playing for hours on the park's playgrounds with their children.

This all changed following the financial crisis of 2007-2008. Yes, the children now were in boarding school, and so, there were no demands at home to distract the couple from their responsibilities at work. But the need for 12-hour days, seven days a week, and both national and international meetings meant that it was rare indeed when the two could find time for each other. A week could go by—sometimes two—when one would be coming home after a night at the office when the other was about to leave for work. Gone were their meals together, either at home or out with friends. The Met or Carnegie? A thing of the past. It would be almost two years before they even could book seats for a Broadway play, and then, Ashley was forced to take a friend when, at the last minute, Tony was called into a board meeting.

Now, here they were, on the telephone, he about to take his life and she pleading with him to reconsider.

"Tony? *Tony!*" she yelled in desperation. "Don't do it!" she again yelled into the telephone.

After several seconds of silence, he spoke quietly, the words almost imperceptible: "I can't do this anymore, Ashley. I'm putting an end to the pain."

"No, Tony, don't do it! Whatever it is, don't do it! Think of the children! What will we do without you?"

"You should have thought of that, Ashley, when you couldn't kick your heroin habit."

"Wheel of Fortune" (Photo: Cheshirskiy Kot, Shutterstock)

"I've seen the tattoo of the Wheel of Fortune she has on her back."

38. Wheel of Fortune

"**So,** did you know Katlyn Lundquist well," asked Special Agent Ron Bishop of the Federal Bureau of Investigation as he took his place next to the sheriff in a front-row pew at Mt. Bethel Church in Columbia, Pennsylvania.

"I guess you could say that," chuckled Police Chief John Packard. "Knew her parents, for sure—Nels and Didrika. Long-time residents of the city. Tragic what happened to them back in '07."

"What happened," asked Bishop, maintaining his gaze on the other mourners who were filing in to pay their respects before the closed casket, many, apparently, silently beseeching the Lord to protect the soul of the dearly departed before they crossed themselves, turned, and found places to sit in the small country church.

"Died in an automobile accident on the Pennsylvania Turnpike in June of that year," replied Packard. "They'd immigrated to the US '94 with Katlyn, who was five at the time, best I recall. She was the sole survivor. Nels was the owner of Lundquist Service Corporation, a successful professional laundry and carpet cleaning firm serving the hotel, motel, and bed and breakfast industries in York, Lancaster, and the surrounding areas."

"Wow, that musta been rough on the kid."

"Well, let me tell you, she had it pretty good right up to their deaths. Fact is, the girl was spoiled rotten. They never disciplined her. Which pretty much explains why she was such a hellion. And the older she got, the worse it became."

"So, she had run-ins with the law?"

"A few?! That, my friend, is an understatement. I first ran into her right after she entered high school. I won't bore you with all the details, Ron, but in her junior year alone I recall charging her with trespass and disorderly conduct, possession of a controlled substance, possession of drug paraphernalia, and public drunkenness."

"Man, you really had your hands full just with her."

"I'll say. Now, mind you, her parents always took care of those problems, which is to say they made them go away."

"What you mean to say, John, is they paid the fines or bought off the parties harmed."

"Well, when they could. When they couldn't, our juvenile court stepped in, so there were some actions taken there. But you couldn't access the records, Ron, because as you know, she being a minor and all, any court proceedings would have been sealed.

"After her parents were killed, she seemed to straighten out for the most part, and we didn't have any major problems with her. But she continued to use fake IDs now and then, usually when she was carded at one of the local roadhouses. The bartenders all knew her, and it became something of a joke with them."

"So, when did she start to go by the name Nicole Davis?"

"I never was sure, Ron."

"Well, that's the name we knew her by in New York City."

"It must've had some special meaning to her. Best I could tell, it's a name Lundquist used since she was a freshman in high school. She had fake IDs made using that name so she could buy alcohol and cigarettes for herself and her friends. When she started driving, she carried several driver's licenses ostensibly issued by different states. She used those whenever she was carded. All of them were fabricated using her picture and the name Nicole Davis."

"So, how do you suppose she came to end up in the New York City area, John?"

"Well, as you know, a little over two years ago, we started having trouble with the mob moving into Lancaster and York. A cartage association run by the Mafia was attempting to take over the garbage, trash, and recycling business in those towns. Basically, the mob established their own trash companies in those cities and then, by talking to the customers of established independent operators, convinced them to shift their business to the mob by undercutting their current trash haulers' prices. One independent operator who fought them was Ryan Belmont. He operated a trash and recycling business in Lancaster with his son, Sanford. They both were found shot to death in

June, 2012. The killer or killers were never found, but it was always assumed the mob was responsible."

"Okay, I understand. But how does Katlyn Lundquist play into that?"

"Well, sir, I heard—and mind you, this is unsubstantiated—she was seen with Jimmie Lupinacci's son, Tommie, a real psychopath if there ever was one, at a nightclub in Pittsburgh on two successive weekends in early September, 2012."

"That would be Jimmie Lupinacci, the mobster."

"One and the same."

"And once you've seen Lundquist, you'd never forget her. She was exquisite. Blonde, svelte, with sculpted facial features, she was a Swedish beauty.

"Oh, yes, I know."

"Apparently, Jimmie couldn't take his eyes—or his hands—off of her. It didn't take long for word of those sightings to get back to us."

"So, you're thinking was that Tommie Lupinacci was behind the Belmont murders."

"No question in my mind, Ron."

"Well, sir, at about the same time all of this was happening, Lundquist suddenly puts her family's home up for sale. She never had to worry about money, so when an offer came in, albeit lowballed according to her agent, she accepted. Then, she sold her car the next day, gave her real estate agent power of attorney, and disappeared.

"Except that's, apparently, where you picked up on her, Ron, if I understand correctly."

"That's right. We'd been watching the Lupinacci's attempts to move into on southeastern Pennsylvania for some time and saw Tommie's new girlfriend as someone we might be able to 'flip' for information. We knew her as Nicole Davis, of course, and easily determined he had put her up in nice apartment on Henry Street in Brooklyn. Given the circumstances, it didn't take too much pressure to convince Davis—that is, Lundquist—to work with us. Basically, we threatened to charge her with conspiracy and other assorted crimes and misdemeanors.

"In the end, she went along with our plan to wire her apartment, tap her phone, and the like, for the purpose of gathering the evidence we needed to take down the Lupinacci family. Secret liaison meetings between Lundquist and one of our agents took place, as needed, in the woman's room in a small diner around the corner from the local tattoo parlor she frequented. As you know, she was into body art."

"I'll say. I've seen the tattoo of the Wheel of Fortune she has on her back. It's the same symbol found on tarot cards. But that wasn't all. The New York City deputy coroner also photographed tats on her back and upper right arm. The lady was a real showcase, that's for sure."

"So, how did she end up murdered?"

"It's clear Lupinacci—who was married, by the way—went to Lundquist's apartment to drink and have sex out of sight of prying eyes. She liquored him up every time he was there, something I encouraged her to do. Hell, he probably even paid for the booze. And given Lupinacci's volatile nature, it wouldn't surprise me if he picked up her phone after having one too many and made calls to North Carolina and Pennsylvania on occasion without even thinking about the consequences. It's only after he sobered up the next morning that he might have had second thoughts about having made those calls—*if he even remembered making them*. It probably wasn't until bad things started to happen—as in the case of several truckloads of his cigarettes being seized—that the connection occurred to him."

"So, he put two and two together—"

"And had her killed," said the sheriff, completing the agent's sentence.

"Yes, we found her dumped in Thomas Paine Park, within spitting distance of 26 Federal Plaza, well after midnight one night. No identification on the body. Her clothes, which could have been purchased at any of a hundred stores in the five boroughs, weren't disturbed, and a preliminary examination showed she wasn't sexually assaulted. One shot in the back of the head. Classic sign of a mob hit."

"Well, I hope she didn't suffer."

"There were no signs of a struggle, John. The autopsy suggested she knew her—"

"Why, hello, Father. Ron, allow me to introduce Father Glenn Everett. He's been watching over our flock for the past 20 years. Father, this is Ron Bishop. He's with the FBI."

The two men rose to greet the pastor. The men shook hands.

"Agent Bishop," intoned Father Everett, "I understand we have you to thank for returning Katlyn to us."

"Well, Father, it was the least I could do, given I feel responsible for her death."

"How's that, Agent Bishop?"

"Well, I keep going over and over in my mind the things we asked Ms. Lindquist to do for the Bureau. On hindsight, I wonder if we didn't push her too far, too fast. But then, there were urgent matters to address regarding the cases we were working on, the deaths that already had occurred in a number of those cases, including some in Lancaster and York, and— Well, I constantly find myself asking the Lord for forgiveness. Butt never seems to be enough," said the agent, shaking his head. "Even now, I wake up, night after night—"

"Agent Bishop—may I call you Ron?"

"Yes, of course."

"Ron, you must always remember the words of Isaiah, Chapter 65, Verse 24: *And it shall come to pass, that before they call, I will answer; and while they are yet speaking, I will hear.* You must take comfort in the thought the Lord already knows what is in your heart."

"Thank you, Father. I needed to hear that," said Ron, tears forming in his eyes.

The sheriff and the agent sat as Father Everett turned, walked to the altar, and with the crowd hushed, began the funeral service.

Preceding Lundquist's interment. Agent Ron Bishop spoke eloquently of Katlyn's spirit and zest for life. "It is because of her dedication to seeing justice done, to ensuring the murderers of many in your area stand trial, that I stand before you today to sing her praises," said Bishop, holding the lectern with both hands to steady himself. "To her, the path she took was not one of choice but of necessity. And for that she paid the ultimate price. Certainly, she will be remembered all the days of our lives as someone truly special. And so, I say to her, rest in peace, dear Katlyn. And may the Lord bless and keep you, forever and ever."

See Endnote 13.

"The Death of Madam Ophelia" (Photo: Pinterest)

It was the loud, incessant knocking on the front door of her establishment that awakened Ophelia Defour from her fitful sleep in the back room of her home behind her tarot parlor.

39. The Death of Madam Ophelia

It was the loud, incessant knocking on the front door of her establishment that awakened Ophelia Defour from her fitful sleep in the back room of her home behind her tarot parlor. The evening's meal of boiled crawfish and corn on the cob went down easily enough, but then, heartburn, accompanied by nausea, set in and kept her awake well into late hours of the night. Now, that knocking at the door not only had startled her, but added to her discomfort.

What in God's name does someone want at this hour," she thought, as she rose, switched on the lamp next her bed, and reached for her robe. *They can't be wanting their fortune read!*

The hammers in the parlor's grandfather clock struck the chimes eleven times.

That anyone even would *think* about using Madam Ophelia's fortune telling services at that hour bordered on the unbelievable. Located in the backwaters of Louisiana, far from the nearest Interstate let alone a major state road, her only patrons over the last several years, all be them increasingly infrequent clients, were Cajuns who had been born and raised in the area and who had grown up in a culture based on superstition, tarot card readings, and other forms of fortune telling. To them, the occult and acceptance of the paranormal was a much a part of their life as eating and breathing. That Madam Ophelia's predications came true from time to time only added to her reputation, lending credence to those who sung her praises.

Was it not Madam Ophelia, asked Sophronia Beliveau, a Cajun who lived down the road in Palmetto, four miles west of the old concrete bridge over the Atchafalaya River, who foretold the death of Philomine Mercier's beloved son, Otis, the big clumsy man everyone called *Grand Beedé?* Otis drowned in the bayou west of Levee Road the morning after Madam Ophelia read Philomine's fortune and warned her of such an event. Truth be told, everyone knew Otis was born under a bad sign, and it was only a matter of time before he'd came to a bad end. The fact is, Madam Roselle had predicted the same outcome some weeks earlier. Chalk one up to Madam Ophelia's timing.

As for her other, many "successes," if Ophelia were to tell the truth, she'd have to admit her readings including huge helpings of gossip scooped up from conversations with other patrons, all of whom couldn't have been more eager to share whatever they knew about their relatives and neighbors, especially if they had been bound to secrecy. And then, of course, there was the counter at Surette's meat market in Lebeau—a crossroads, of sorts—where news changed hands as quickly as did the smoked pork flung across the countertop! Talk about your grist for a fortune-teller's mill. Surettes was the Mother Lode . . . all of which made Ophelia a star of sorts among the locals when it came to tarot card readings.

The hulking, rusty neon signboard next to the road at the entrance to the long driveway leading to Madam Ophelia's Tarot Parlor had seen better days. Electricity no longer coursed through its glass veins to ignite what might remain of the noble gases that once announced the parlor's location in garish pink, green, and blue colors:

MADAM OPHELIA
TAROT READINGS
FORTUNE TELLING

The sign had died a slow silent death over the last decade. It was a portent of things to come for the entire fortune-telling "industry." Many early 21st century adults rejected what they thought was a charade while others, who took some comfort believing the future could be foretold, had turned to various fortune-telling sites available on the Internet or their cell phones. It was a different era, to be sure.

Leaving the comfort of her bed and donning her robe, she walked into the parlor, switched on a lamp in the corner, approached the front door, switched on the porch lamp, and peered through the peep hole. What she saw was a was a man nattily dressed in a black pinstripe suit, light blue shirt, and red and black stripped tie. A red silk handkerchief blossomed from his suit jacket's left front pocket. From all appearances—including his white hair and thick-lensed, horned-rimmed glasses—he was George Burns incarnate.

"Can I help you," Ophelia shouted through the closed door?"

"I'm here to read your fortune," the man shouted back.

"Read *my* fortune?" Ophelia responded, not understanding what she had heard.

"Oh, yes," said the gentleman. "Be not alarmed, Madam Ophelia, I mean you no harm. But after all these years of reading the fortunes of others, I have been sent here tonight to read *your* fortune."

Ophelia shook her head. Surely this was a dream . . . it must be the boiled crawfish and corn on the cob "speaking" to her, she thought. She vowed then and there *never* to make another meal of the two ingredients.

"Sent here by whom?"

"I wouldn't even give that a thought, Madam Ophelia. Just think of my being here as an extraordinary event someone experiences only once in their lifetime."

Ophelia still wasn't convinced. But the gentleman persisted, indicating he would take no more than a few minutes of Ophelia's time. Then, he would be gone, leaving the same way he came.

Try as she might, Ophelia could *not* for the life of her see how the man had even arrived at her door in the first place. No car or other type of vehicle could be seen parked in the circular drive to the front of her establishment. Still, given his entreaties, his gentlemanly manner, and the impeccable way in which he was dressed—not to mention her curiosity—Ophelia unbolted the door and ushered the man into her parlor, where she invited him to sit across from her at a large oval table covered with a heavy dark cloth—the table at which she had read the fortunes of others for more years than she could remember.

"May I?" asked the visitor, picking up the deck of well-worn 22 major **arcana** tarot cards. He shuffled them over and over again with his eyes closed as he hummed softly to himself. After what seemed like an eternity—but what in reality was not more than a minute or two—he stopped, put the cards in front of Ophelia, and asked her to cut the deck, which she did. Then, he dealt five cards face down on the table in the form of a horseshoe. From the gentleman's vantage point, the five cards represented, in order from left to right, Madam Ophelia's *Present Position, Present Desires, the Unexpected, the Immediate Future,* and *the Outcome.*

Setting the deck to his left, the visitor reached for the first card, Ophelia's *Present Position.* Slowly, he turned the card over. It was *The Fool.*

Ophelia pulled her robe around her neck as if she had felt a chill and looked into the visitor's eyes. *What did he know that she didn't,* she wondered?

"I see an interesting woman in front of me, who, as a girl on 15, acted with spontaneity and lived in the moment, a woman who did the unexpected and acted on impulse. She took crazy chances. She felt carefree, uninhibited. She took a foolish path, and gave birth to a little girl—"

Ophelia gasped.

"You're surprised?" asked the visitor, rhetorically. "Oh yes, there are no secrets that can be kept from me. I know all. Unlike you, I know everything: past, present, and future. Your child—the little girl you named Angelica—was given up for adoption on the day your parents sent you to live here, with your aunt, Cezelia, from whom you inherited this business. At midnight tonight, Angelica's daughter with give birth to your third grandchild, who will be named Emeline . . . and a sweeter child will ne'er be found."

At hearing this, Ophelia clasped her hands to her face and burst into tears. Her life lay bared before her.

It was Billy Hardwick, she recalled to herself, who had lured her into his father's barn, not that she wasn't more than willing to climb the rungs of the old wooden ladder to the loft that late summer's night with him in hot pursuit. The smell of new-mown hay was intoxicating, as were the sweet words Billy kept whispering into her ear as they lay side-by-side, listening to the cicadas in the trees outside.

Billy, a senior and captain of the high school football team, was all of 6-4, blonde, and blue-eyed. He was, unquestionably, the most sought-after boy in school. That he even had paid attention to Ophelia, a sophomore, much less had asked her to the movies, puzzled her at the time. Yet, there they were, fresh from a double feature, lying together, she very much infatuated with him. The two beers they shared, which Billy had found in the refrigerator at the back of the barn, only heightened their emotions. Within moments, Ophelia was transformed from a giddy school girl into a woman.

A month later, when she missed her period, she realized how foolish she had been. By then, however, it was too later. Her parents sent her to a home for unwed mothers and, upon the birth of her daughter, who was put up for adoption, immediately packed her off to live with her mother's sister in Louisiana. Ophelia never saw nor heard from her daughter again.

The visitor waited for a few moments before turning over the second card, Ophelia's *Present Desires*. It was the *Eight of Wands*.

"Ah, yes," proclaimed the visitor. "How fitting this is, fitting indeed. I see a woman who is about to make a major change in her life, someone who is about to finish something up, end a chapter, bring something to a conclusion."

This is strange, thought Ophelia. *I know things are changing. How many times have I thought my days as a fortune teller may be numbered? And how often have I wondered what I would do when I no longer had people coming to me to learn their fates? Now, here I am, and a stranger, no less, is telling me that a major change is about to happen in my life. This can't be a coincidence.*

She sat back in her chair, looked to her left side, and appeared to be deep in thought.

Meanwhile, her visitor sat back, reached into his suit jacket's inner pocket, and, pulling out a small cigar travel holder, and asked: "Would you mind if I lit one and enjoyed a brief smoke?"

"What? What did you say?" asked Ophelia, who, startled, now had turned her attention back to the man seated across the table from her.

"I was wondering if you might permit an old man the pleasure of lighting up a cigar and enjoying a few puffs before we continue with your reading."

"Oh, of course not. My first husband smoked cigars. I rather enjoy the scent of fine tobacco. Here, let me fetch you an ashtray."

With that, she rose, went to the walnut cabinet at the wall behind her, selected a heavy glass ashtray, and brought it to the table. "This should do," she said, setting it in front of him.

The man selected a fine Cuban cigar from his holder, pulled a butane torch lighter from his vest pocket, snapped the ignition button, and with the cigar held down at an angle to the flame, turned the cigar in his fingers while he inhaled using short puffs until the end glowed cherry red. Then, he took the cigar out of his mouth, turned it around, and gently blew on the glowing end to ensure it had been evenly lit. Returning the lighter to his vest pocket, he sat back, took a puff, and sent a halo of white smoke Heavenward. After taking a few more puffs, he set the cigar on the ashtray, leaned forward, and revealed the third card, representing *the Unexpected*. It was *The Devil*.

"This is interesting," he intoned. But it does explain a lot about how you've been feeling of late . . . seeing the world turning colder, perhaps even foreseeing a bleak future. Oh, yes, I know. You've accepted what's been happening around you, in many ways allowing yourself to be controlled by the life you've chosen for yourself. But I assure you, all that will change by the time I leave here tonight."

Ophelia appeared to brighten at this prospect. This man, who seemingly came out of nowhere, knew more about her than did anyone on Earth with the exception of her parents. And now, he appeared to be giving her some hope that her life was about to change, not in the days or weeks ahead, but *tonight . . . tonight, by the time he leaves*. She let out a sigh of relief and looked with anticipation toward the reading of the next card.

Madam Ophelia's visitor reached for the fourth card, the one representing *the Immediate Future*. As he turned it over, they saw *Judgement*. "Ah yes, the lone wolf, the one who is running away." Before continuing to his reading, the visitor picked up his cigar, took a puff, and carefully laid it on the ashtray.

"Yes, *Judgement* . . . the card of rebirth and absolution. For it is a day of reckoning, Sister Ophelia, a day to be released from your guilts and sorrows, to forgive yourself as you would forgive others, and in doing so, atone for your past mistakes. Unburden yourself, my dear . . . feel your sins washed away, for the feelings your have are those of salvation. When the angels call, you will be reborn and can begin anew. *Judgement* shows that renewal is at hand."

Ophelia took a deep breath, then slowly let the air out of her lungs. Turning her head to one side, she nodded several times with a sense of finality. *Yes, she thought, it's time to forgive myself. I've made mistakes, of that there can be no question. But what's done is done. There's no going back. Tomorrow will be a new day.*

And then, the gentleman reached across the table and turned over the fifth and final card: *Death*.

"I am *Death*, Sister Ophelia. It *is* Judgment Day, when the faithful are brought to Heaven and their sins forgiven.

"Be not afraid, but come with me now. Death is inevitable, and the events of tonight are inescapable."

■ *Theodore Jerome Cohen*

Endnotes

1. The Doves Type

 ❡THE DOVES TYPE® is Robert Green's digital recreation of the Doves Press Fount of Type.

 Original type conceived, commissioned & directed by T. J. Cobden-Sanderson, London, 1899.

 Developed by Emery Walker, assisted by Percy Tiffin, at Walker & Boutall, London, 1899 — 1900.

 Punches cut by Edward Prince, London, 1899 — 1901.

 Produced in a single size, 2 Line Brevier (16 pt), by Miller & Richard, Edinburgh, 1899 — 1905.

 First sorts delivered October 1899, full fount of characters completed July 1901.

 Punches & matrices thrown into the River Thames by T. J. Cobden-Sanderson, March 1913.

 Entire type dropped into the River Thames by T. J. Cobden-Sanderson, August 1916 — January 1917.

 Digital facsimile Doves Type® developed 2010 — 2015.

 OpenType Version 1.0 released December 2013. Version 2.0 released January 2015.

 Created using sources from original Doves Press publications & 150 metal sorts recovered from the River Thames by Robert Green & the Port of London Authority salvage team, October & November 2014.

 The Doves Type® — www.dovestype.com

 Distributed by Typespec Ltd — www.typespec.co.uk

2. Judgment Day

This story was inspired by the play *Steambath*. It is the second play by American author Bruce Jay Friedman. It was first performed Off-Broadway at the Truck and Warehouse Theater, where it opened on June 30, 1970, closing on October 18, 1970, after 128 performances.

This play presents the afterlife as a steam bath, in which recently deceased souls (who may not in every case realize that they are dead) continue to obsess about the same petty concerns that obsessed them in their lives. Ultimately, they are cast into another room offstage that is represented by a dark void by God, the steambath's Puerto Rican attendant, with the help of his assistant, Gottlieb. In the play, the new arrival, Tandy, at first refuses to accept what's happened, and when he finally does, he pleads to be allowed to return to his life. *Steambath* was controversial when first produced for its obscene language (which was softened for its television version), its satirical take on religion, and some brief nudity.

Friedman claims to have been inspired to write the play in part because of a "bad experience with the food at a Chinese restaurant" that had him contemplating mortality.

The play was then produced for PBS in 1973 with José Pérez playing God, Bill Bixby playing Tandy, and Valerie Perrine as the blonde bombshell Meredith. Only 24 PBS affiliates carried the program.

Steambath became a series on the cable network Showtime in 1983 starring Robert Picardo in the Tandy role, Janis Ward as Meredith, Al Ruscio as DaVinci, Rita Taggart as Blanche and Allen Williams as Gottlieb. José Pérez reprised his role as God, who now also had a name, "Morty." (A pilot was produced and aired, later followed by five additional episodes.)

Along with *Oh! Calcutta!* the play was spoofed as "Bathtub" in *The Odd Couple* episode, "What Does a Naked Lady Say to You?"

Barnes, Clive (July 1, 1970). "Theater: Anthony Perkins Directs 'Steambath'; Friedman Casts Deity as a Bath Attendant". *New York Times*.

Friedman, Josh Alan (September 23, 2009). "Steambath". *Black Cracker Online*.

A tip of the hat and many thanks to Sandy Rangel, Audience Services Volunteer, WETA TV & FM, Washington, DC, for generously sharing the information above.

3. A Final Goodbye

Sultana on fire, from *Harpers Weekly*.

Sultana was a Mississippi River side-wheel steamboat. On April 27, 1865, the boat exploded in the worst maritime disaster in United States history. She was designed with a capacity of only 376 passengers, but she was carrying 2,155 when three of the boat's four boilers exploded and she burned to the waterline and sank near Memphis, Tennessee, killing 1,192 passengers. This disaster was overshadowed in the press by other events surrounding the end of the American Civil War, most particularly the killing on the previous day of President Lincoln's assassin John Wilkes Booth.

4.   Cursed

An excerpt of this story was submitted to *Indies Unlimited* on September 15, 2018, in that organization's Flash Fiction competition:

"Blood Moon" (Photo: K.S. Brooks)
Indies Unlimited, September 15, 2018

5.   Stacked Pebbles

This story was submitted to *Indies Unlimited* on September 22, 2018 in that organization's Flash Fiction competition. The subject matter is controversial, so Ted submitted it under the pen name Josiah Stone (no pun intended).

6.   Grand Entrance

This story is based on "The Luthier of Ozone Park," which can be found in Ted's book of short stories, *The Road Less Taken: A Collection of Unusual Short Stories – Book 2:*

https://www.amazon.com/dp/B01MSO1LND

7. Chauncey

Missy, actually, is Missy Cohen, the eldest daughter of Ted. Chauncey is her beloved dog of many years. They both reside on Manhattan's West Side, near Riverside Park, where they converse daily on their many walks.

8. Wet

This story is based on the discovery of the B-25 Mitchell Bomber pictured below that was found at the bottom of Darwin Harbour.

B-25 Mitchell Bomber that crashed in Darwin Harbour, carrying two Australian and three Dutch airmen.

https://www.abc.net.au/news/2018-01-05/b25-mitchell-bomber-which-crashed-in-darwin/9306472

9. Watson's Lake

This tale is based on a true story, the details of which can be found here:

http://tahltan.ca/loretta-frank-yukon-woman-still-missing-after-25-years/

10. Shady Brook

This story was submitted to *Indies Unlimited* on February 2, 2019, in that organization's Flash Fiction competition. The photo prompt for the competition was of the walkway pictured below:

"Walkway" (Photo: K. S. Brooks)
Indies Unlimited, February 2, 2019

11. Stefan

This story is adapted from the fictionalized autobiography of the author's life as a violinist. Titled *Full Circle: A Dream Denied, A Vision Fulfilled*, the novel can be found in eBook, paperback, hardcover, and audiobook formats at Amazon, B&N, Kobo, and other booksellers worldwide.

http://www.amazon.com/dp/B002YNSC88

12. Stakeout

This story is adapted from Ted's novel *House of Cards: Dead Men Tell No Tales*. This is the second book in the Detective Louis Martelli, NYPD, mystery/thriller series of six books. The novels may be read in any order. The books can be found in eBook, paperback, hardcover, and audiobook formats at Amazon, B&N, Kobo, and other booksellers worldwide.

https://www.amazon.com/gp/product/B07J2XFRVP/?ie=UTF8&%2AVersion%2A=1&%2Aentries%2A=0

13. Wheel of Fortune

This story is adapted from Ted's mystery/thriller *Wheel of Fortune*, the sixth book in the Detective Louis Martelli, NYPD, series. You can find more information about this book (and series) at:

https://www.amazon.com/gp/product/B07J2XFRVP/?ie=UTF8&%2AVersion%2A=1&%2Aentries%2A=0

■ *Theodore Jerome Cohen*

About the Author

Theodore Jerome (Ted) Cohen is an award-winning author who has published more than ten novels—all but one of them mystery/thrillers—as well as two books of short stories and eight flash fiction anthologies in the series <u>Creative Ink, Flashy Fiction</u>. He also writes illustrated storybooks for children (K-3) in the series <u>Stories for the Early Years</u>. Dr. Cohen holds three degrees in the physical sciences from the University of Wisconsin – Madison. During the course of his 45-year career he worked as an engineer, scientist, CBS Radio Station News Service (RSNS) commentator, private investigator, and Antarctic explorer. What he's been able to do with his background is mix fiction with reality in ways that even his family and friends have been unable to unravel!

Dr. Cohen's writings (he holds three degrees in the physical sciences from the University of Wisconsin – Madison) have received the highest reviews from Feathered Quill, Hollywood Book Reviews, Kirkus Discoveries, Pacific Book Review, Reader Views, and Readers' Favorite, among others, with many of his books recognized for their excellence through medals awarded by several of these same organizations following their annual book competitions. In 2017, for example, Readers' Favorite awarded Dr. Cohen's first short story anthology, *The Road Less Taken: A Collection of* Unusual *Short Stories - Book 1*, a Silver Medal while the National Association of Book Entrepreneurs (NABE) awarded the same book its Pinnacle Book Achievement Award for Best in Category: Short Stories. A member of the Society of Children's Book Writers and Illustrators (SCBWI), Dr. Cohen's articles often can be found in that organization's *BULLETIN* as well as in *Story Monsters Ink* magazine.

From December 1961 through early March 1962, Dr. Cohen participated in the 16th Chilean Expedition to the Antarctic. The US Board of Geographic Names in October, 1964, named the geographical feature Cohen Islands, located at 63° 18' S. latitude, 57° 53' W. longitude in the Cape Legoupil area, Antarctica, in his honor. And given he is an avid communicator (Dr. Cohen has been a licensed Radio Amateur since 1952, and holds an Amateur Extra Class license (call sign: N4XX)) and an accomplished violinist (he played with the Bryn Athyn (PA) Orchestra from 2007 through 2013), it is not unexpected that stories involving the Antarctic, radio, and music are to be found throughout his writings.

In addition to his adult and childrens books, Dr. Cohen writes Young Adult (YA) novels under the pen name Alyssa Devine. His YA novel *The Hypnotist* (Lexile® measure 930L) currently is in the Core Genre (Mystery) Reading Program at Neshaminy High School in Bucks County, Pennsylvania, where he is a guest lecturer on the subject of mystery writing.

Finally, from March 1966, through March, 1968, Dr. Cohen served as a Captain in the United States Army, Corps of Engineers.

Dr. Cohen and his wife, Susan, live in southeastern Pennsylvania, not far from where Washington crossed the Delaware River to surprise the Hessian forces in Trenton, New Jersey, on the night of December 25-26, 1776. Visit Ted at <www.theodore-cohen-novels.com>.

■ *Theodore Jerome Cohen*

55831815R00102

Made in the USA
Middletown, DE
18 July 2019